OF ARROWS AND ROSES

A VISANTHIAN NOVEL

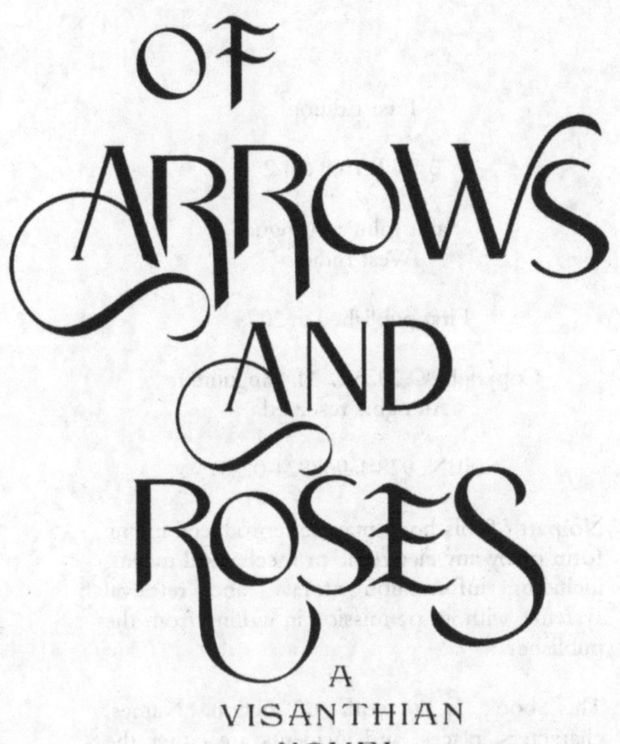

THERE'S DARKNESS
IN ALL OF US

OF ARROWS AND ROSES

A VISANTHIAN NOVEL

L. M. SANGUINETTE

First Edition

3 5 7 9 10 8 6 4 2

Saint John's, Antigua
West Indies

First published in 2025

Copyright © 2025 L. M. Sanguinette
All rights reserved.

ISBN: 978-1-968824-02-0

DEDICATION

To those who believe that love transcends lifetimes.

TABLE OF CONTENTS

Glossary

Argia – People of Fire
Harri – People of Earth
Iturri – 'Source' or the god of Visanthe
Kanala – One who channels an element
Visanthe – The world of elemental magic
Visanthian – A person hailing from Visanthe

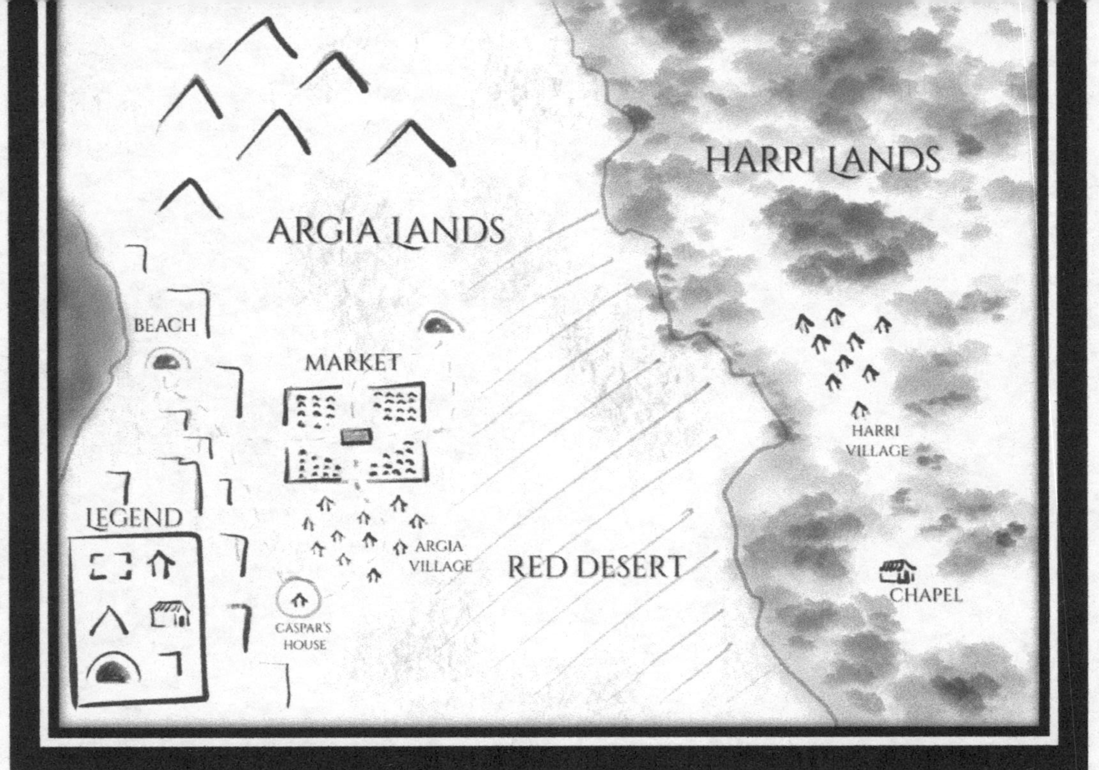

ARGIA LANDS
HARRI LANDS
BEACH
MARKET
HARRI
VILLAGE
LEGEND
ARGIA
VILLAGE
RED DESERT
CASPAR'S
HOUSE
CHAPEL

⚜ CHAPTER 1 ⚜

CASPAR WOKE TO THE SOUNDS OF THE
waning night. The cooing of the desert owls and the fading
moan of the wind might have offered solace to people
whose beds would keep them warm for another few hours.
But not to him. Another waning night meant another day in
poverty, and potentially worse, another fruitless hunt.

He strapped his bow and quiver onto his back and
tucked his hunting knife into his tunic before sneaking out
into the dawn. He rounded the house, peeking through his
father's window on his way to the edge of the desert. His
father lay sound asleep, curled up in wool blankets, well-
protected against the cold of the desert nights.

Still sleeping, good. These days, Caspar preferred leaving
before his father got up. That way, he wouldn't have to hear
him complain of the way the heat ate at his bones or the
hunger-induced headaches. He slipped away quickly,
quietly. The only voices that chased him were the ones in
his own mind.

Their house was a hovel, large stones slapped together and plastered with painted white clay. It held up during the limited rainy season and provided enough protection from both the heat and the cold of the desert. The rain gutters dangled freely from the wooden pagoda, torn off in the last of the sandstorms and unfixed ever since. They had money once, before his father's injury. Time, too, in his mother's life. Now they had neither, and each day brought new hardships.

The stars above him began to fade, but the rising sun was still lost below the horizon. It was time to go. Caspar pulled up the cloth at his neck in preparation for the roaring, sand-laced winds and set off down the trail. If he was lucky, he'd find a desert rodent or two in the nearest plateau and be back before the morning markets opened; otherwise, it was going to be another long day.

Caspar followed the dusty trails from his village through the weaving canyons that had long since dried out under the harsh sun. What little life remained was sustained on the few creatures that still deigned to call this wasteland home. On days like today, when the rains were still months away and hunger in the village was at its peak, Caspar cursed the burnt sienna trails and blackened, skeletal tree trunks that spoke of a life that must have once thrived here, as though the lands themselves were scarred and damaged. Still, this was his home. He'd never seen anything but the rising canyons and red sands. He'd never known anything but the scorching days and freezing nights under cloudless skies. He'd never been beyond the desert.

The first hour of his search had been in vain. The morning sun had already crossed the horizon, and he had nothing to show for it but a light coating of dust on his clothes and in his hair. But Caspar would not be deterred. He made his way farther across the plains until his home canyon was completely obscured by the horizon. He'd never wandered this far from home before.

Still, time ticked on.

Off in the distance ahead of him, he spied the rising treetops of the forest, where the desert gave way to the *Harri* territories. His father had warned him never to cross into their lands; they were uncivilized warriors. On a good day, Caspar wouldn't have even considered it, but today was no good day. The sun was already high, burning his forehead and bleaching his auburn locks bright red, and he couldn't come back empty-handed.

Caspar raised his forefinger and thumb to the sky. *Just going on eleven,* he thought. He scanned the length of the empty horizon, searching for some semblance of movement, but found only the rising ripples of heat from the dusty red plateau. *Father will wonder what's taking me so long with today's hunt.* Caspar reasoned the best course of action would be to turn back and see if he could trade one of his knives for some basic ground provisions and, if Mr. Nesim was in a good mood, maybe even a jackalope. Those might last a week if they were careful, and with that, he would have another few days to tend to his own grounds before having to hunt again. But the fire in his stomach had not been put out by the blazing sun above, and the stark contrast of the green trees with his own red soil called to him. His bare feet carried him across the sunburned lands to the place of which he'd only dreamed.

The world seemed to know the contours of each territory better than any man. A harsh line in the ground, marked on one side by barren soils and on the other by damp grass, signalled the end of his own *Argia* lands and the beginning of those of the *Harri*—people of earth. *How curious,* he thought as he bent down to touch it. The earth beneath the blades of well-nourished grass was also damp. Perfect for crop-growing and tending livestock—*and wild animals would have plenty to eat, too.*

Caspar took a deep breath and crossed, waiting for some sensation or warning that he should turn back now while he still had the chance, but none came. There was no sign of an attack, no strange mists, no tingling in his shoulders. Other than a refreshing shade from the sun, Caspar felt no difference between the two lands. He let out a soft smirk. *Only bedtime stories, then,* he realized as he remembered his father's warnings.

Caspar pulled out his knife and began etching Xs into the trees to guide his return. The deeper into the forest he wandered, the more the grass gave way to mud, and the darker the world around him became. The trees grew to heights he'd never seen before, some of their trunks growing as thick as three full-grown oxen. The dense canopy above protected the ground below from the sun. Now and again, patches of sunlight shone onto vibrant green grasses, but mostly the ground was filled with strange bulbous plants and the occasional rotting tree trunk.

Just my luck, he thought as he marked another tree. Caspar was well out of his realm of knowledge in these woods. Some bushes appeared up ahead, filled with large, brightly coloured fruits. He knew better than to pick without knowing, so he scanned the floor for traces that other creatures had been foraging too—discarded seed pods, half-eaten fruits, even the animals themselves would've been a big help—but he found nothing.

Best leave it be, he decided.

Under the darkened canopy, it was hard to tell the time of day. Caspar felt like he'd been walking for hours and knew he should be heading back, but it irked him to do so empty-handed. He dropped onto his hands and knees, scanning the grounds for signs of life. He imagined tracking an animal in the forest was like tracking one in the desert. No matter the terrain, all creatures leave tracks. But, aside from his own heavy footprints, these grounds seemed untouched. Caspar was beginning to wonder if the forest was really inhabited at all, when a large *thud* sent a cacophony of feathers fluttering into the skies.

He prickled.

Another *thud.* And another...

It sounded like the falling rocks in the canyons, but Caspar couldn't imagine where such a noise could be coming from.

Another *thud.*

Caspar crawled through the bushes, keeping as close as possible to the ground, in search of the source of the noise. He hoped it was an animal. Something *that* big would surely keep them fed and might even put money in their pockets. He could even spend time caring for his father's illness rather than going on these hunts. Caspar stood up behind a tree, pulled an arrow from the quiver and nocked it into his bow.

At the sound of the next *thud,* he fired, the arrow finding its home in something most definitely alive, but *not* a creature—or one he could eat. It dropped to the floor with a soft crash and wailed, sending more birds into the skies, before it called out with a teary voice, "Who's there?"

It was a woman's voice.

Casper had no clue what to do. He turned back to his stream of X's, knowing that the only person he might encounter in these woods was a *Harri*, and that, if he did, he would be in trouble. The ground beneath him trembled.

"Show yourself, you coward!" she continued with more grit. He heard the *snap* of his arrow and the soft clatter it made as it hit the floor. Caspar contemplated her request, hearing his father's chastising voice even as he stepped out of the shadows. At first glance, she looked like a wild creature. Her dark hair was tangled and full of leaves. Her eyes were rimmed with smudged black kohl, her legs strong and sturdy between the slits of her long green tunic that had muddied at its hem. "At whom do you think you are blindly firing—" She stopped suddenly as if the sight of him set her on edge. She clenched her bloodied arm and growled at him ferociously. "*Argia*. Stay away from me!"

"I'm sorry," Caspar began, looking around the young woman for the source of the noise. "I thought you were an animal."

"Whatever would've given you that idea?" she hissed, tears framing the side of her face, though she refused to let her strength waver. Judging by the state she was in and the terrified look in her eyes, Caspar thought his assumptions were not too far off, but he knew better than to make the comment.

"I heard loud sounds... too loud to be coming from someone your size. Let me help..." Caspar stepped towards her, but her good hand flew up automatically in defence.

"I said stay away from me!" Pebbles lifted from the ground and flew towards him violently. He dodged just in time to avoid a large one aimed at his head.

Caspar's jaw dropped. He'd never seen anything like it

before. The woman had raised the earth with nothing more than a twitch of her fingers.

"You're *kanala*," he called back in disbelief, his own fear causing him to raise his bow again.

The *kanala*, or so his father had told him, were the few people in this world blessed with control over the elements. Their legends said that the great spirit of the land, *Iturri*, poured itself into a select few at birth, allowing them to manipulate the element of their homeland. Caspar had only ever seen the *Argia kanala*, the ones of his land who wielded fire. Their powers usually required the presence of their given element, which made him more cautious of the strange, earth-wielding girl, as she was at no loss for prime material.

"Don't hurt me…" he gulped, nocking another arrow into place.

"Me? Hurt you?" the girl replied in disbelief. "You're the one going around shooting blindly at whatever creature has the misfortune of taking a breath in your vicinity." She tried again to sweep up a wave of pebbles, but her good hand shook. She began to sway on her feet, and Caspar realized the blood had begun to pool beneath her.

"You're losing a lot of blood," Caspar remarked, replacing his arrow and lowering his defence. He looked around tentatively, searching for another spark of human life. But his search came up empty. No rustling bushes, no smoke, no lights, no telltale signs of a village anywhere. "What were you doing out here all alone?"

"I'm fine…" she tried to growl, but the sound faded as her voice trailed. "You shouldn't be here."

"Neither should you…" Caspar took a tentative step towards her, but she retreated. Her damaged arm trembled as tears pooled in her vibrant green eyes.

"I'm warning you. Stay away…"

Caspar stared at the trail of blood streaming from the gash he'd left in her arm. She was *Harri*. Worse still, she was *kanala*. He shouldn't feel sorry for her. How many times had his father told him they were heartless creatures? How many times had he warned Caspar not to stray from the desert?

But this girl, though tattered in dress and prickly in person, didn't look as evil as his village had painted her people out to be. On the contrary, she looked more afraid of him, especially masked and holding his bow and arrow.

Caspar rested the bow gently on the ground and replaced the arrow into his quiver before taking another cautious step towards her.

"I'm not going to hurt you," he said as he removed the cloth he used to cover his nose and mouth from the harsh desert sands.

Aside from her heavy breathing, her body was still. Her eyes widened as though she'd seen the spirit of *Iturri* before her. They traced the lines of his body, and then his no longer covered face. A curious part of him wondered what she saw—if she questioned, as he did, whether the person before her was man or monster.

The next step he took closed the distance between them. Up close, Caspar caught a whiff of the iron-tinged scent of blood, and just beneath it, the scent of lavender. She might have looked a mess, but doubt began to creep in. She was no savage creature of the forest. She came from a somewhere. She was a someone. He made sure to move slowly as he reached over to wrap her arm.

The girl stared incredulously at the cloth. "What are you doing?" she scoffed as she recoiled from his outstretched hand.

"Helping you."

"Why not just finish me off? I'm *kanala*, remember? Big, bad, scary *Harri kanala* who will attack when provoked and kill you without a second thought… Isn't that what your kind says?" Spite filled her voice.

"Yes," he admitted bluntly. "But you're also a person, and you're bleeding out."

She frowned at the cloth; heavy black brows furrowed over the most vibrant green eyes Caspar had ever seen. They glowed the colour of sun-hit leaves, startlingly different from his own and those of his people.

"It's dirty," she grumbled.

"So are you."

"How dare…" She stared woozily down at her tunic. Whatever she was about to say remained on the tip of her tongue. With a bite of her lip, she relented, shifting nearer to him, and offering her trembling, bloodied arm.

The arrow had only skimmed her arm, but the gash it left was enough to send a waterfall of blood down to her wrists. She was lucky he'd missed the bone.

Caspar wrapped the cloth around her with care. She winced as he pulled it taut and shifted away from him, but Caspar held her firm. "It's got to be tight if you want it to work."

"You didn't need to help," she said as she cleaned the rest of the blood on the draping part of her tunic, leaving a large red patch that would surely stain the green fibres brown permanently.

"I'm not a monster."

"I'm hardly sure of that," she growled with a pointed glance at her blood smear. "Flailing your flying daggers everywhere…"

"What were you even doing out here anyway?" Caspar asked as he gazed around at the empty forest. "You must be miles away from any kind of civilization…"

"I was practising," she added bitterly. "But I doubt I'm going to be able to lift anything bigger than a pebble for a while." She slumped down, resting her back on one of the sturdy tree trunks.

"I'm sorry…" Caspar mumbled. His father would've considered it a triumph to have downed a *kanala*—especially a *Harri kanala*—but Caspar doubted whether his father had ever met a *Harri* before. This woman—bitter as she was—didn't seem like the life-sucking, sub-human creature that his father and the rest of the village had made them seem. She actually seemed *normal.* "Why weren't you practicing closer to home?"

Her eyelids fluttered closed. "Not that it's any of your business, *Argia*, but people like me aren't allowed to practice."

"*Kanala?*"

"Women."

"Oh…" He blushed. "I didn't—what are you doing?" he asked, noticing her droop.

"Resting…" she replied finally, but her body had begun to tremble.

A soft dip in temperature told Caspar it was time to leave. The afternoon would soon turn to evening. He would return empty-handed and probably have to explain where all the blood came from, but it could've been worse. *He* could've been the one injured.

He thought of his father and the limited rations left behind. It would be garlic soup for dinner, again. He would have to write this day off as another fruitless hunt, but at least this strange adventure would be over. Whatever twisted dream he'd fallen in to would end as soon as he was back on his native red soils. No one would ever need to know where he had gone and what had transpired…

Caspar was about to leave when he turned to her again, half slumped against the tree and breathing heavily. The sound of it gave him pause. If he left her here, she'd soon faint from loss of blood, and then she'd fall prey to whatever beasts truly hid in this wood. Caspar looked around for other signs of humanity, but something told him they were the only two people around for miles. His lips curved into a sorry frown as he contemplated her again. Anyone else from his village would've left her—anyone else from his village wouldn't have come this far, to begin with.

But Caspar had never been like his people.

❧ CHAPTER 2 ❧

KEZIAH AWOKE IN AN UNFAMILIAR AND uncomfortable bed to a sharp pain in her arm and the scent of something sweet. On a table beside her sat a chipped porcelain teacup that might have once belonged to wealth, but in its current state, she figured was probably bought in a second-hand marketplace. Steam curled over its worn gold lip. Whatever sweetness lay within sauntered up her confused nostrils and caused her mouth to salivate.

Steadying herself to sit was no easy task. Keziah could hardly move her right arm due to some uncomfortable swelling, but she managed to prop herself up against a firm clay wall.

No headboard, she noted irritably.

Keziah lifted the teacup to her lips with care though it rocked in her unpractised left hand. The steaming, pale green liquid was as sweet as she'd imagined and unexpectedly sharp, burning its way down her throat, but it was too good to stop. Her muscles relaxed but the throbbing in her arm was still as present as ever. She replaced the teacup and looked down at the mostly fresh bandage that was already blooming a blood rose.

"Shit," Keziah swore under her breath. "How am I ever going to explain this one?" She made to remove the bandage but touching it sent a sharp pain down her body. She winced, having disturbed whatever scab was forming beneath the cloth. Now, even the slightest movement of her fingers hurt more than anything she'd ever experienced.

Harsh, unfamiliar words from behind the door made Keziah jump. They reminded her of both the inconvenience and uncertainty of her situation. She still had no idea where she was, but judging by the décor of the room, she was no longer in the *Harri* provinces. Keziah lifted herself out of the uncomfortable bed with difficulty and crept over to the door. She could hear two men yelling about something, but the words sounded muffled through the wood. She pressed her ear to it in hopes she would catch more than incoherent yelling.

"How dare you! You ungrateful little…" a heavy voice began before a bout of coughs interrupted him.

"Father, I know what you think but—"

"No. Their kind is not to be trusted. They are manipulative, land-abusing monsters. I cannot believe you brought one into my house!"

"I couldn't just leave her there. She would've been a fresh meal for any larger creature lurking in that forest."

"Good. That's one less of them roaming around out there."

"Father, she is a person."

"You know nothing about their kind."

Keziah had heard enough. She thrust the door open,

coming face to face with the man that had shot her, and another older man who Keziah assumed was his father. The man stared blankly at her. His father scoffed in her direction before limping with the assistance of a wooden cane into another room.

"You're up," the man remarked.

"Upset you can't kill me now?" Keziah replied bitterly.

He frowned. "If I had wanted to kill you, I would have left you in that forest."

"No, that's right. Instead, you brought me to a land full of ignorants and murderers," she hissed. She didn't dare hide the disgust in her heart. Manipulative? Land-abusing? Keziah turned up her nose. She had never been so insulted by another person in her entire life. "Point me to the door, I am leaving."

The man let out a resigned sigh, as though he were trying to justify to himself why she needed to stay. Well, if it were up to her, Keziah would not have even deigned to visit this ridiculous little hovel of a house. She had no plans to be a burden to a stranger, let alone one who couldn't decide if his decision to save her life was a good one or not.

"You cannot leave in the condition you are in," he replied finally, though she could tell he wasn't truly convinced by his own words. The man cast a glance over to the room his father sat in. "My father is quite tame compared to the people of the village… They won't stop at words alone if they see you out and about. It's not safe."

"Then why bring me here in the first place?!"

"I…" he began but quickly thought better of it.

"Point me to the door," she hissed through gritted teeth.

He did as she asked, without question. Keziah marched past him in the direction of the door, confident of each stride. There was no use exchanging more words with him or his father. She was halfway out the door when she felt a sharp, unbearable pain streak from her arm to the base of her foot. The debilitating sensation prompted a scream. "Ouch!" she cried and turned to find the man clenching her wound between his muscled fingers.

"Present situation aside, I have no intention of hurting you," he said calmly. Before she could counter, he added, "I only wish to see you healed."

Keziah bit down on the tears prodding at her waterline as she looked from him to the wound on her arm.

"It is the least I can do."

Keziah was stubborn, but she wasn't stupid. She'd hoped that these people weren't the prejudiced and ignorant people her father had told her of in her youth. But her hope seemed to have been misplaced. Based on the conversation she'd overheard between him and his father, and what he'd said of his town, she reasoned leaving alone would get her harassed at very least—or worse. Plus, after seeing his reaction to finding out she was *kanala,* she knew she would be seen as a serious threat. In which case, her life was in greater danger than she'd initially thought. The best course of action, she figured, was to lay low until she regained full use of her powers.

"Fine," she said with a resigned huff, tugging her arm away. He released her quickly, but the feel of his touch lingered on her skin.

"Stay until you are healed." He dropped his gaze, unable to meet her eyes. "Like I said, it's the least I can do for…"

She raised a pointed brow. "Shooting me?"

"Yes." He bit his lip. "The bedroom is yours for as long as you're here."

"I have no intention of getting comfortable in this wasteland," she growled, raising her chin in defiance.

"As you wish…"

"I do."

The man dragged his hands over his face and groaned.

Frustrated? Well, at least we have that in common, she thought.

Instead of barking back at her, as she would've expected, he was calm, measured, and even gracious with her.

"There's a small stream out back for you to rinse off in—if you'd like. I'll find you some clean clothes and then make another pot of tea. You should probably rest up. You lost a fair bit of blood."

Keziah caught a glimpse of her reflection in a worn-out mirror. She looked like she'd been through battle. A red dust coated her skin and hair. She smelled too. A quiet guilt crept into her heart as she realized she would not get to enjoy her Tante's fresh homemade lavender soap. *Oh, Tante…* Her heart sank even further at the thought of her family. How would she ever explain her disappearance? Would her father send out a search party? And if he did, would they even know where to look?

Her mind was racing. At this point, she knew the bath would do her good, regardless of the soap. Back home, she relished in baths for thinking and clearing her head. Granted, she imagined her bath was much more luxurious than whatever this boy had to offer, but at the end of the day, a bath was a bath.

Keziah reached her good hand up to the crown of her head and pulled a twig from her tangled black hair. As she twirled it between her thumb and forefinger, she felt her stomach twist into knots. She was going to be in serious trouble when she got home. Besides, if anyone caught a glimpse of her injury, they might start an unnecessary war—and that was the one thing she did not believe in.

With a long, exasperated sigh, Keziah nodded. When she did return home, it would be prudent to do so in the best state possible, as to avoid any unwanted altercations.

The boy bobbed his head in reply, a hesitant smile forming at his lips. It was a shy half-smile, as though he were out of practice. She noticed something like relief wash over him, loosening his shoulders and relaxing his stance.

No one had ever reacted to her like this. She would've expected more of a challenge, but this boy really did look ashamed of his actions. She thought back to their encounter in the forest. He had been startled by her, afraid of her powers, yet he still bandaged her wound. Whatever possessed him to bring her back here was a mystery, but he at least seemed to have some sense of morality. Some justice flowing through those *Argia* veins.

Prejudice aside, he looked as though he really did wish to help her. Keziah knew better than to let her guard down entirely, but the softness in his voice and his smile was disarming.

"Out of curiosity, how did I end up here?" she asked, scanning the walls and the world beyond the windows, searching for any hint at where in the world they were, or even how long she'd been gone from home. "Wherever here is..."

"I carried you," he replied, a faint blush creeping over his cheeks as he strolled over to a door at the opposite end of the room.

"You?" she whispered, contemplating his lanky physique with a tilt of her head. He didn't look like much, but she reasoned there were muscles hiding under the long white tunic. There had to be. Otherwise, there was no way he would've made it anywhere with her on his back.

"Yes. Are you coming?"

Keziah pursed her lips, holding strong to her reservations about him, but obliged him, nonetheless. She followed close behind, avoiding his father's murderous gaze. The boy pushed open the door, ignoring his father completely, but Keziah moved cautiously. Even without looking at him, his hatred made her skin crawl.

As they passed his room, she felt the icy contempt rippling from him. The old man glowered at her the entire length of the house and as she followed his son out into the back garden—if one could even call it that.

Keziah was glad to be out of the suffocating air of the house, but the stifling heat of the desert village was no better. She raised her good arm overhead, blocking the harsh sunlight from her eyes. In her own village, light was at a premium. It first had to filter through a dense canopy before reaching their cold stone pathways. Even in the clearings, the warmth of the sun came as a welcome hug.

This sun was different.

The garden was a prime example of this. Cacti sprouted between mounds that might have once belonged to lettuce beds. Thorns and brambles lined the exterior walls. Everything she saw had been scorched by the desert sun and coloured a burnt orange or brown—a far cry from her own home, which was covered in green leaves and vibrant flowers as far as the eye could see. The garden was practically screaming for help in a hoarse and dried out voice. The whole thing looked in dire need of water and care.

"I'm Caspar, by the way," the boy said, snapping her out

of her contemplation.

"Keziah," she replied, turning to find him staring at her. "What?"

"Strange name."

"So is yours," she scoffed.

"It's nice though," he added, provoking a traitorous blush from her.

Don't be ridiculous, she scolded herself. *What do you care that a poor boy thinks your name is nice…*

She looked away from him at the hovel, and then at the vast desert sky beyond. Somewhere beyond the hollowed-out blue expanse was her home. Her forest. Her people. How far was she from home? From the people who knew and loved her? And then another treacherous thought appeared… Had any of them ever complimented her name?

Remember, he is an Argia, he hates your kind… a little voice called out from the crevices of her mind. It felt so familiar, yet she knew it was not her own. It belonged to her people, her history… Her father.

"Are you alright?" he asked, noticing her distant gaze.

"I was promised a bath," she replied.

"Right…"

The boy, Caspar, led her to the secluded edge of the would-be garden where the so-called bath lay in wait. He stopped at a wall of rock that towered high enough over them to provide a little shade.

Keziah stared at the promised bath—a stream, little more than a trickle of water from a groove in the canyon wall. It was not enough to lather and soak her skin. Barely enough to rinse the mud and blood from her body.

"What do you expect me to do with this?" she asked, disdain littering her words.

"Bathe," he replied. "In that bucket, you'll find a bit of soap," Caspar added as he handed her a towel from a nearby clothing line. "I'll leave some clean clothes on your bed. If you need anything, I'll be in the other room."

Keziah made for the strange bucket when the scent of something familiar stopped her in her tracks. She froze as she took in another whiff. "Is this… lavender?"

Caspar nodded.

"Where did you get lavender?"

He blinked at her as if she'd asked where the dirt came from. "It grows here. Under lots of sun and thin soil. You should know that. I smelled it on you when we first met."

"My Tante makes soap out of it, but…" she lowered her tone innocently and added, "I assumed it came from our lands."

Caspar raised his eyebrows at first and then grinned. "Not all flowers are grown in environments of abundance. Sometimes, the sweetest ones are grown in adversity."

"I didn't take you for a poet," Keziah said.

"I'm not," Caspar replied. "It's what my mother used to say before she died."

"Oh." Keziah wished she'd put a boulder in her mouth.

She had an awful way with words, always saying things harshly and directly, confronting everything head-on rather than with care. In conversations with her people, it didn't matter as much. They were all just as stubborn and direct. But speaking with Caspar felt… different. He seemed so diplomatic about everything.

Unlike his boulder-headed father, she thought.

Keziah felt ashamed of how she treated him, despite only knowing him for about an hour. She searched for an appropriate response, for a way to soften her words, but none came. Perhaps she was not made for such things.

Caspar looked back at the tangle of weeds and mounds of forgotten soil and smiled, as though he saw something she didn't.

"Don't worry about it," he said nonchalantly. "That's a story for another day."

I don't plan on being here more than a day, she would've said, but if he knew she planned to sneak out after dark, he might keep a closer eye on her. Instead, she nodded and made to take off her tunic.

Caspar blushed and turned his back to her.

"As I said, if you need anything, I'll be in the house." And without another moment's hesitation, he strode away.

"Embarrass easily, huh?" Keziah said as she stripped down with great difficulty to her bare brown skin. She rested her tunic on one of the rocks beside the stream and stared at the bloodstained splotches. "My favourite tunic…"

She knew she couldn't be seen in it again, especially not with the stained fibres. She'd have to commission another one from the seamstress when she got back to the village… And possibly bribe her with fruitcakes to not mention anything about the blood to her father. With her good hand, Keziah dabbed a bit of the lavender suds onto the splotch, hoping it might diminish the stain if left to sit.

In the meantime, she went to work on herself.

The cold water soothed her muscles and formed droplets between the hairs on her arms and legs. Under the desert sun, she wondered how the water remained so fresh. It must have come from somewhere deep underground, or else a reservoir. *Did the desert people have reservoirs?* she wondered. Regardless, the cold water was a blessing. She gave thanks to Iturri for the small kindness as she splashed her face.

Keziah dipped her fingers in the bucket again and brought them to her nose, closing her eyes as she relished in the scent. The sudsy concoction that Caspar had shown her smelled better than any of her Tante's finest soaps. Stronger too. She took her time, lathering her skin and letting it sit, hoping to come out smelling as strong as the plants themselves.

It had only been a day since she'd last bathed, but she was coated head to toe in a layer of dust and muck that made her feel as though she'd spent months away from water. Keziah closed her eyes. As she lathered her face with her good hand, she remembered all the times she'd tried to lift that stubborn rock in the woods. After many unsuccessful tries, she'd taken to jabbing at it, breaking off chunks of it and tossing them to the ground.

He said he'd heard a large animal, she thought with a smile. *Just wait 'til my arm heals. I'll send that rock flying, and it'll sound like a herd of animals.*

Once the rest of her body was cleaned, Keziah tried pulling at the bandages again, wincing like before, but at least this time she knew to expect the pain. She unravelled them with care, rinsed them in the stream, and set them to dry in the sun. The healer in her village would have some sort of pulverised plant to put on it that would heal it in a day or two. She'd seen it used on the soldiers. But Keziah was a far cry from the healer, and she knew nothing about this new desert flora. She hoped that Caspar might have something similar. He seemed resourceful enough, and whatever tea he'd left for her earlier had brought her strength back almost immediately. The next thing she had to worry about—aside from her arm—was finding food.

Her stomach was beginning to talk.

Keziah rewrapped the bandages and covered herself with a cloth before heading inside. For now, she was safe. Her own father would kill her when he found out where she'd gone. That was, at least, if Caspar's father didn't kill her first.

❧ CHAPTER 3 ❧

"THEY'RE WHITE," KEZIAH GRUMBLED AS SHE glowered at the cotton tunic and trouser set he'd laid out for her.

Caspar looked from her to the garments and raised his eyebrow. "And?"

Keziah crossed her arms. "They're plain. I don't like them."

"It's not like you're in much of a position to choose…"

"They have no personality. I don't like them. I will not wear them."

He let out an exasperated sigh. *What in the world have I gotten myself into?* he asked himself. Here she was, both a guest and a stranger in his home—brought here out of the goodness of his heart after having the misfortune of getting injured—and she was complaining about clothes… Had no one ever taught her gratitude? How could she be so superficial as to reject assistance on the basis of taste?

Caspar wondered if all the *Harri* were like her, arrogant

and demanding. He crossed his arms, mimicking her disgust. They were so very different. Maybe taking her in was a mistake. If they couldn't see eye to eye on something as trivial as clothes, he couldn't imagine them ever getting along.

Just until she's better, he reminded himself. *Then she'll be on her way, back to whatever palace she came from, and you can get on with your life like before, without fear of retaliation.*

He'd planned on making it out to the market alone for food before she'd woken up, but his father had made that plan impossible. Because of him, Caspar now felt obliged to drag her along, inconvenient as her presence would be. He would've left her in the house if he trusted her not to escape, or his father to not pick a fight he was in no way capable of winning. This way at least, despite the inevitable risk, he could keep an eye on her.

All you've got to do is keep her from prying eyes… And from making a scene. If that means you have to pacify her… so be it.

He took a deep breath, centring himself before he addressed her again. "Like them or not, they'll reflect the sun. Besides, if anyone sees you in that dyed getup of yours, they'll know you're not from around here."

"I think they'll know just by looking at me," she retorted, gesturing to her ebony locks and vibrant green eyes, which were a far cry from the traditional *Argia* features. Where his skin was the colour of parchment, hers brandished the warmth of cinnamon bark. Where his eyes shone a feline's yellow, hers glowed green like burning copper. And of course, her dark cape of raven-black hair would stand out among the sea of coppery blondes.

She was right. A little coloured clothing would be the least of their worries.

Caspar thought maybe a shawl from his late mother's untouched wardrobe would do. He walked over to his father's room and, ignoring the grouchy old man's complaints, pulled out a plain white shawl lined with tassels from his mother's wardrobe.

As he was about to return, he caught a glimpse of another one peeking out from behind other fabrics. He tugged it out from the bottom of the wardrobe. This one was a darker red with intricately woven designs of stars and other shapes. He couldn't remember if he'd ever seen his mother wearing it—though, to be fair, he could hardly remember his mother at all. It was admittedly beautiful. A work of quality craftsmanship. Yet another trinket from the world of wealth they'd long since been privy to.

Caspar slung them both over his arm and walked back to the room, hoping Keziah would appreciate the choice when, in fact, he had no doubts as to which she'd choose. To no one's surprise, when he held both options up to her, she snatched the colourful one before he could even get a word out. At least it would work to cover her distinguishing features, and then there was the bonus of stopping her from complaining about the white robes.

He bit down on the grin at his lips. She was nothing if not true to herself, a trait he admired greatly in others.

"Well… it's not much, but at least this way they'll have to look twice before deciding you are different," he said, pleased that he finally got her to stop moaning. "Now, hurry up. We're going to find food. I'm almost surprised that you grumble more than your stomach."

Keziah rolled her eyes. "I did not ask to come here."

"If I had known you were going to be this much trouble, I would've left you in the forest…" Caspar mumbled.

To his surprise, she looked almost disheartened at his words. His stomach twisted. Had he been too hard on her? She turned from him, hiding her growing disappointment. He seemed to have offended her, but he had no idea how or why. Still, there was a prickle in his chest that made him want to say something—anything—to take back his words, to erase the hurt.

"Well, I'm here now," she scoffed. "And unless you plan on taking me back yourself, I am not going anywhere."

Even though she turned her nose up at him, Caspar could hear the disappointment in her words, weaving its way between each pause. He uncrossed his arms, his own heart caving a little as he watched her, but no further words crossed his lips. He wouldn't even know where to begin with an apology. Besides, Keziah seemed intent on ignoring him.

She let the silence hang between them, the unfinished argument lingering in the air.

Before Caspar could get another word out, Keziah discarded her towel. It fell, pooling at her ankles, suddenly. Intentionally.

Caspar felt his entire face blazing with embarrassment. Almost as quickly as she'd dropped the towel did his gaze hit the floor. He felt his pulse thundering in his ears. It took every ounce of strength he had within him to keep his eyes fixed on the stone. Even the closeness of her ankles to his gaze sent his mind reeling. He wasn't sure what unsettled him more—the way she was perfectly unbothered by her state of undress, or the sharp, unexpected jolt of attraction that shocked his system. It hit like a bolt of lightning. He swallowed hard, his mouth suddenly dry as he tried to rid his mind of those mere seconds of exposure.

He dug his nails into the palms of his clenched fists, trying to regain control of his body.

"What?" she smirked, taunting him as she dawdled in getting clothed. He could tell she was doing it to mock him. "Never seen a woman before?"

Not one who looks like you, he thought. He gritted his teeth, hoping to stop any stupid comments from slipping out. He sucked in a breath, feeling his heart pounding harder against the hollows of his chest. Its rhythmic beat echoed in his head like chapel bells, though there was nothing saintly about his thoughts. What little he did manage to see in those brief seconds had already etched itself into the crevices of his mind. She was so astonishingly different from anyone he'd ever known…

As he turned his back to her, he felt the burn of her gaze on his shoulders. She watched, waiting for a reaction from him. He wouldn't give her the satisfaction.

"Would you get dressed already? You could at least try to be a bit more modest…" he growled.

Keziah snorted. "Where's the fun in that?"

Her taunting voice sent shivers down his spine. He listened out for the sensual swish of fabric gliding over skin. Keziah took her time, elongating each move for what he imagined was the simple pleasure of seeing him suffer. She may not be *Argia*, but she certainly had a fire about her.

Suddenly, Keziah tapped him on the shoulder, causing him to tense up further.

"I'm dressed," she assured him, though her tone had shifted once more. The irritation and haughtiness had returned. "Now what?"

Caspar turned to find her swathed in the billowing white fabric like a true desert queen. Her eyes were laced with challenge and shimmered more vibrantly than the green leaves of a thousand spring trees. He gulped. Something about seeing her in his people's clothes did not provide the relief from tension he'd hoped. Despite their modest shape, they did nothing to tame his heart. His palms began to sweat…

I must be coming down with a fever, he surmised as he secretly wiped his hands on his trousers. He would keep their trip to the market short, or as short as possible, to be back in time for a nap.

As he worked to regain composure, Keziah tied her hair into a long braid, pinned it into a low knot at the back of her neck. She draped the shawl carelessly over her head in a way that he knew would slip in no time.

"Here," he said, only managing to get out the solitary word. Caspar stepped towards her cautiously, taking hold of the edges of the fabric and wrapping it gently around the contours of her face. He tied it and hid the knot, adjusting it so that it shaded her eyes without blocking her vision. She gazed up at him as he worked, equally silent as she contemplated him. With each unintentional meeting of their eyes, Caspar felt his chest tighten.

What had she done to him?

When he was finished, Keziah moved over to the mirror and contemplated her appearance. She tugged at the tunic until she was perfectly content with the fit.

"I suppose it will do," she said as she played with the fabric.

"You're quite the princess, aren't you?"

"Weren't you rushing me, *Argia*?" she replied, casting an indignant glance in his direction. "Your insults will only keep us here longer."

She marched out of the room and towards the entrance.

Caspar let out a resigned sigh. This woman was going to be the death of him. He took a final glance in the direction of his father's closed door, wondering only for a second if he should've heeded his warnings, before following Keziah out into the street.

* * *

The vibrant colours, loud shouting, and sharp scents of the marketplace were an assault on all senses. From one stall, multi-coloured spices filled the air while its neighbour brandished cuts of exsanguinated, hanging meats. Others had perfumes next to bakeries, metal trinkets next to freshly dyed carpets, tanned hides next to caged livestock. Hagglers and vendors yelled back and forth between each other. People moved in and out of the market in droves. The stained dust of the market floor never settled—and neither did the patrons.

Caspar led Keziah through the weaving maze of market stalls, having to drag her from the fine silks and ornate metalworks. She stopped at every stall with expensive and eclectic trinkets on display. Even the stands with brightly coloured fruits and finely cured meats were not safe from her. Caspar could tell her taste was exquisite, even for things that were entirely foreign to her. He wondered what kind of life she must have led to have developed such preferences.

"Don't speak to anyone," he cautioned Keziah as they manoeuvred through the stalls.

"Don't treat me like a child," she chided him.

He closed his eyes and shook his head. *Why did I get myself into this...*

As they drew closer to their destination, a small, hidden trader's stall at the edge of the market, Caspar felt his heart sink low in his chest. It wasn't the kind of stall you sought out under good circumstances.

But necessity knows little of morality.

A gilded knife weighed down both his pocket and his heart. It was one of the last things that remained from the time when they had more, had enough to not wonder at where their meals were coming from. Back when his mother was still alive… Memories lingered in the unpolished hilt that made it harder to let go of. But he'd returned with nothing from the prior day's hunt, and as a result, a sacrifice had to be made—painful as it was to do.

"How much for this?" he asked the stall attendant—a portly, unkempt man by the name of Mr. Nesim. He wasn't the shadiest of characters in the market by any means, but that didn't make him a saint either. The old man had been after his knife for some time, knowing of its inherent value.

Caspar had usually brushed him off, content in the fact that a good hunt would bring in enough to sustain them. But he'd had no luck for weeks now, and their stock was officially depleted—that, and there was another mouth to feed. Now, Caspar hoped he'd be willing to pay a sum that would fetch at least a few days' worth of meat, unsure when he'd be able to make another hunt.

He twirled the knife in his fingers, contemplating it fondly before resting it on the table before the man.

Mr. Nesim looked up at him with a mischievous smile. "So, you've come back…"

"That's beautiful!" Keziah exclaimed, her eyes glued to the shiny metal trinket.

"It is, isn't it?" said Mr. Nesim. "You have a good eye, little one."

Keziah furrowed her brow as she stared up at him.

"Where did *you* ever get something so nice?" she prodded, as if she'd thought he'd stolen it from somewhere.

"It was a gift," Caspar growled through gritted teeth, annoyed that, once again, she'd ignored his request.

He didn't need to be reminded of how nice the knife was. Keziah prattled on about the quality of the metals and the engravings. Mr. Nesim humoured her, complimenting her intelligence patronizingly, but Keziah didn't seem to pick up on it. A vein ticked in his jaw as he listened to the two of them, wanting to—for some reason—demand that he show her more respect. She was right of course. She knew surprisingly more about forging than he'd imagined, more than even he did.

Keziah spoke of the craftsmanship required to do engravings in such detail, even the quality of the metals used, as if she'd been there the day they were pulled from the mine and witnessed it forged firsthand… The more she spoke of it, the more it pained him to let it go.

But what choice did he have?

It was either that or pray for a decent hunt—which, in this particularly dry season, was akin to starvation. And there were now still three mouths to feed.

"I'll give you five silver pieces for it," said Mr. Nesim condescendingly.

"Five? Last time you offered me ten!"

"Yes, but times have changed, my boy. The days are hotter, not as easy as they once were…"

"You're not really considering selling it, are you?" Keziah interjected, ignoring the customary haggling of the market. "Especially not for five silver pieces…"

Caspar leaned over and whispered in a low growl, "I'm trying to get ten actually."

"No, no. The lady is right," Mr. Nesim replied, trying to seem reasonable. He rubbed his greedy hands together. "I should do a bit more. How about seven? Seven will get you a ration of goat at the butcher's, maybe even a loaf of bread if you ask nicely."

Caspar stared at the finely sharpened steel, the gold and silver hilt, the labyrinthine designs of stars and suns and other things his mother once rattled on about at great length, and to which he wished he'd paid more attention. Would his mother forgive him for selling her prized possession? Even if it was in the name of taking care of the family? How could she not? At the same time, he found his hand gripping the hilt tighter than before.

"I wouldn't part with it for less than twenty," Keziah's blunt voice chimed, snapping him out of his daze. "Unlike some of the trinkets I've seen in the other stalls, this is genuine gold from the volcanic soils in the minor *Harri* territories, the steel is finely crafted in the Idune style. The piece itself is a work of craftsmanship. It's a wonder why you have such a thing at all."

"Now see here," Mr. Nesim began, but quickly corrected the harshness of his tone, *"Ya haram,* you must be mistaken." Caspar doubted she understood the meaning of the word, for if she had, she might have lunged at him for his patronizing label. "A knife like this one is pretty, but it is not worth that amount. The steel is worn. The hilt needs polishing and looks chipped. I'm not even sure if it's real gold..." Mr. Nesim continued, but Caspar had stopped listening to his insults.

"You know it is, you old stump," he heard Keziah call back before the barrage of voices appeared in his mind.

She was rude, but she was right. He couldn't part with it.

Quality aside, he was too attached. He wouldn't sell it—he couldn't.

"You sell it to him for seven today and by tomorrow it'll be hanging in the stall for twenty-five," Keziah whispered to him.

It pained him to admit he knew she was right, but that didn't change anything. They still had to eat.

"Keziah, I need the money to buy food for—"

"Food?" she practically shouted to the heavens. "If this is all for a little food, I have a better idea, and one that won't lose you a trinket you're so clearly uninterested in parting with."

Suddenly, without hesitation, Keziah dragged him by the sleeve, back through the weaving market stalls, leaving Mr. Nesim calling out higher and higher numbers. His voice only carried so far. Soon, it was entirely muffled by the sea of shuffling patrons, and then even that faded as they left the limits of the town. She pulled him decidedly towards the point where society peeled away, on towards where village turned canyon.

❧ CHAPTER 4 ❧

CASPAR STARED AT THE DARK, GAPING CAVE
mouth before him in awe. The desert behind them baked in
the sun, its sands rippling like gold silk in the midday winds.
The ground beneath them was cracked, as if begging for
water. There didn't seem to be any life around for miles.

So, why had they come? And, even more concerning,
how did she find this place?

Keziah, a complete foreigner to his lands, had managed
to lead him to a cave he'd never seen before. She'd dragged
him along the market pathways and then to the outskirts of
the village to where canyons grew from the ground like
towering trees. She'd paused a few times along the way,
pressing her ear to the rocks that were deeply embedded in
the ground, and tapping at canyon walls. The first time she
did it, he'd wanted to ask if she'd gone crazy, but she'd
shushed him before he could get a full word out. It was as
though she was listening to something but, for the life of
him, he couldn't imagine what.

Standing before the mouth of the cave, he worried she'd lost her mind.

"Why are we here?" he asked, now that she'd finally stopped pressing the side of her face to every rock in sight.

"Smaller creatures like the dark. They can hide better from their predators." She raised a brow in challenge. "Shouldn't you know that *Mr. Hunter*?"

Normally, he wouldn't bother with the small creatures. They provided little sustenance and were difficult to catch. But Keziah had dragged him out here with such fervour that he felt bad to dismiss her without seeing it through to the end. Besides, she was adamant.

Caspar rolled his eyes. "I have… But have you never encountered small predators?" He cast a furtive glance at the floor beneath them, searching for any signs of danger. "Vipers, scorpions…"

Keziah blinked at him. "Don't invent words just because you're afraid. Besides, we aren't going in, you cowardly fowl…"

He wanted to refute the point and let her know that vipers and scorpions were very *real* things—and things that should be feared—but before he could, she shot her hand out to stop him. Keziah etched a large circle into the ground in front of the cave with her heel. She admired it briefly before getting to work on it. At first, she thrust her good hand up into the air a few times, as though she were grasping at some invisible thing above them. Sweat formed at her brow. Whatever she was doing was taxing her body, though he couldn't see the point in it.

"What are you…" he began to ask, when the words caught in his throat.

Caspar's eyes widened.

Suddenly, the dirt moved—of its own volition—through the air, as though it were being scooped from the circle and onto a heap beside it. He took a shy step backwards.

That's right, he remembered. She was *kanala*. The earth bent to her whims. She was a force akin to nature—one to be reckoned with.

Latent fears rose in the shallow filling of his chest. With the beat of his heart ringing in his ears, Caspar began to wonder if he'd been wrong about her, if it had been a mistake to follow her out to a place where no one would hear him scream… A nervous sweat dripped down his brow.

In his mind, the circle began to look like a grave.

"I… I think we—" he began, but Keziah cut him off with a vibrantly disarming smile.

"Okay, get ready," she said eagerly, unaware of how much fear had filled his heart in those few torturous minutes. "Are you okay? You look as pale as a withered plant."

"I…" Caspar's words failed him once more. When she'd looked back at him, he noticed a change in her, a vivacity he'd never seen before. Her skin glowed, shimmering like a bronze statue in the afternoon sun. She moved less incumbered, falling into a routine ease, and even wincing less than before. It was as though using her powers had helped her, had soothed the ache in her arm. He lingered in a daze, still contemplating her long after she'd stopped.

"What in Iturri's name are you gaping at?" she scoffed as she rested her good hand on her hip.

Caspar shook off an embarrassed blush. Had he really been *gaping*?

"I… Umm… What? Nothing," he stuttered. "What am I getting ready for exactly?"

"Right…" Keziah dropped to her knees and rested her ear to the ground. "Just keep your eye on them, we don't want any getting away."

"Any *what?*"

Using her head and bust for balance, she slapped her good hand on the cracked canyon floor as though she were beating a drum.

It took a second but, sure enough, the ground responded with a low growl. It was slight, only a shallow trembling. It followed the rhythm she'd laid out for it, but the earth seemed to magnify the ripples. With each consecutive hit, the ripples grew stronger, until they threatened to throw even him off his balance.

Caspar shot his hands out to steady himself. He remembered a similar tremor in the forest. Back then, he'd believed it was the movement of animals and not a single girl trying to break a rock. A strange feeling started to take root in the pit of his stomach. He couldn't decide if he wished to attribute it to respect or fear—most likely both.

After a few seconds of rhythmic pounding, Keziah shot to her feet. For a moment, all was still again. But then, a smile tugged at the side of her lips.

"Let's see just how good you are with that knife," she said.

"What do you mean…?" he began to ask, when his eyes caught on dancing pebbles beside his feet. The rumbling of the ground returned, stronger now. It came from somewhere deep within the cave. This time, it followed no rhythm, rather urgency. It was scattered and violent; it sounded like a stampede.

A cold sweat broke out at his brow. His muscles tensed as he positioned himself for a fight.

What have you done?

Suddenly, rodents larger than any he'd seen scattered about the desert appeared from the mouth of the cave. Plumes of dust kicked up from their haste followed them out, obscuring his view. Caspar squinted, trying to make out figures through the haze. He slashed blindly, but his knife met nothing. It took a second before he realized his prey were disappearing—no, dropping. On a closer look, he noticed the rodents falling head over foot into the deep pit, with no means of escape.

The pit had been a trap all along.

"How…?" Caspar asked, staring dumbfounded at the pit of prey that was about to save them from starvation. He couldn't manage more than a single word, still trying to figure out how this strange girl with the questionably eccentric taste had stumbled into his life at the time when he'd needed her most. He gazed at her in awe, the coloured shawl doing little to shade the sparkle in her eyes.

Who in the world are you?

"It was nothing," Keziah replied, raising her chin higher as she brushed off the praise. "I could feel their scurrying, so I led them this way."

"Nothing?! This is amazing!" he exclaimed, forgetting their dynamic momentarily as he swept her off her feet and pulled her in for a wholesome embrace. He spun her around in the air, relishing in the happiness of the moment until a different excitement took over. Caspar found himself enjoying the feel of her body against his. Her skin was soft, plush. And oh, for Iturri's sake, she smelled so sweet. The lavender clung to her from the morning's shower. He thought he could lose himself in her, in the embrace... It took him a moment to realize that he already had. When he finally snapped out of it, he quickly put her down and turned away from her. "I, uh—I mean, thank you."

"Yeah, I guess...it is. Isn't it..."

Caspar hadn't the heart to turn around and see her after his accidental outburst of appreciation. He had no idea what had come over him. It just...happened. She was standing there, the glow of the desert creating a halo around her... He hadn't been able to help himself; she'd looked like a saint.

Stranger still, when he'd held her, it was almost as if his body...relaxed. And then she'd hugged him back... Hadn't she? By the time he did look back to confirm, she'd already put distance between them. *No...* he thought. Perhaps he had gone too far...

Caspar held his shoulders upright, reminding himself that it was better to keep his distance. They were too different. Nothing would happen between them. It couldn't. It wouldn't work. Besides, he didn't want anything to happen between them. Right?

He decided not to linger on it any longer, turning his focus instead to the scurrying rodents below. In total, fifteen of them had landed themselves into the shallow grave.

Caspar tore off a dead branch from one of the spindly tree trunks, playing around with its weight. It would work to carry the day's haul back to the house. He tried to distract his mind with the thought of what dishes he could make with such a catch—broth with the bone marrow, sausage with the blood and intestines, and of course the meat, cooked, dried, seasoned. They would have more than enough to eat for the month ahead.

And it was all thanks to her…

He sighed, feeling oddly disappointed. It was no use. It was as though his mind wanted to linger there, in the memory of their embrace. Something in those brief seconds had changed for him. He stole the occasional glance at her, finding himself unable to keep his thoughts at bay. But Keziah hid her face each time he looked over, avoiding his gaze entirely. In truth, she was silent for the rest of the day, offering little assistance in the way of carrying their catch. Even the snarky remarks he'd come to expect of her were mute.

Caspar hadn't spent this long with a woman's company in a long time. He couldn't tell if he'd done something to upset her, or if this was just how she was. Perhaps it was the unexpected hug. It had offended her, perhaps even disgusted her, and with good reason. They had not been friends before that point, and they certainly weren't now. Regardless, something in him had changed, broken, irreparably so.

They made their way back in silence, save for the sound of the crunching gravel beneath their feet. The sound, an echo of the strange feeling in his heart.

Caspar made sure they followed off-beaten paths to keep them away from prying eyes. At this time of day, he expected few people to be outside but figured it was better to err on the side of caution. Now that the markets were closed, Caspar was unable to hide how much Keziah stood out, even in her disguise. She'd fiddled enough with the scarf to have it slip from her head, exposing her burning black locks to the sun. He hadn't said anything about it at the time, having been too afraid to break the silence. Instead, he simply chose a route that would avoid the town entirely.

By all accounts, the desert sun was at its peak and no one in their right mind would be outside in this heat—the irony was not lost on him either. Ever since he'd met her, Caspar was anything but in his right mind.

To his surprise, their path had taken them past some boys playing in the upper canyons. He recognized them by their uniforms; they were soldiers in training. His muscles tensed. He'd seen the way they tormented the younger kids. Compassion and tolerance were not part of their vocabulary. They were people born of resentments and hatreds, people who clung to tradition because, even though it had wronged them, they desired nothing more than to be recognised by it. They were the kinds of people who excused away abuse and violence with training, the kind that might take it out on innocent bystanders—like her.

They were the last people he'd wanted to encounter, especially with her at his side.

Unsure of how she would react to another unexpected touch from him, Caspar simply shuffled closer. He had hoped to keep her shaded with his height, but the boys had spotted them. They might have ignored him entirely had he been alone, but the presence of a girl at his side was an invitation for comments.

"*Yallah*, look what we have here..." called one of the older boys.

Caspar moved closer still, protectively so. He didn't want trouble, but he wasn't opposed to a fight if that was what was required. He did his best to ignore them, and Keziah, following his lead, did the same. But soon, curious leers turned to crude remarks.

"Oh, look eh, he found himself a girl. Now he thinks he

is better than us."

Keziah curled in towards him, going as far as to wedge herself under his arm. He could feel her trembling.

In his mind, the boys were just being hooligans, but something about their remarks seemed to draw out the fear in her. Caspar considered the visuals of their partnership, his chest tightened at the thought of his family being further outcasted by his actions, but looking down at her again, all prejudices fell flat. Right now, she wasn't a *Harri*, she was a girl—a scared one at that.

He tucked her under his arm and kept her shielded.

"It's alright," he mumbled. "I'm not going to let anything happen to you."

He'd said it easily, not giving too much thought to the way his words might affect her. After all, she was a person who deserved to feel safe in this world—a sentiment he had demonstrated to her multiple times since their encounter, and one he hoped she would finally acknowledge. He wasn't much, wasn't special, but he was a man of his word. And though given simply, he would keep his promises to her, no matter the cost.

The boys' jeering faded the further down the path they got, but Keziah remained pressed against him. She fell in tune with his steps with ease. Perfectly, in fact. So much so that, although their walk was surrounded by silence, by the time they returned home, their bodies had spoken volumes.

❧ CHAPTER 5 ❧

FOR SOMEONE SO NICE, ALBEIT A LITTLE TOO modest, I refuse to understand how Caspar earned himself such a vile creature for a father, thought Keziah as she stared stoically at the grumbling man in the foyer.

She had never been the most likeable person, not even in her own village. Usually, people regarded her with the respect maintained for the chief's daughter and nothing more. Keziah knew this about herself. She was exceptionally stubborn and easily picked arguments over minor things. She'd never been quite bothered by people's opinions of her before, but, for some reason, Caspar—and his father, by association alone—were different.

His father, whose face was initially bright and cheerful upon seeing his son, turned sour and cold as his eyes landed on her. His lips flattened into a harsh line that matched the wrinkles above his heavy brow.

"It's still here," he mumbled.

As are you... she wished to say but held her tongue.

Better judgement would see her as being reasonable. She cared not about better judgement. She did, however—and for reasons beyond her—care about Caspar.

"Father, we spoke about this already," said Caspar with an equally cold tone of voice. He took hold of her good hand and squeezed in reassurance. "She will be staying until she is better."

Keziah looked up at him, brows furrowed, unable to hide her confusion. Caspar's sudden change in demeanour caught her off guard. In the little time she'd known him, he'd never taken on such a stern tone or stance. And, more curious still, it was directed at his own father, not at her.

His father's eyes widened. It seemed she was not the only one surprised by this version of Caspar.

"Looks fine to me…" his father replied, his lip curling in disgust.

"Show me the way home and I will gladly leave," Keziah growled in response. Reassurance be damned. His father be damned. She would've gone in an instant had Caspar requested it. In fact, she was itching to get out of this hovel of a house and their ignorant town.

But then, she felt Caspar's hand tighten over hers again. She looked down at his grip on her. The corded veins at his wrist were on full display. Something in her knew he wasn't going to let anyone touch her, hurt her. He wasn't going to let go—not unless she asked.

Unless…he wants me to stay…?

When he moved next, she followed without hesitation.

"No," Caspar said, his voice firm, his conviction unwavering. "I will not hear a word against her." He strode up to his father confidently, adding in whisper, "Besides, she's the only reason you're eating tonight. If you won't show gratitude, you can at least share a roof."

His father was left gaping irritably, but Keziah paid him no mind. Her heart felt as though it had tripped over itself. It stumbled and clattered against the hollow of her chest. It took its sweet time getting back up, too. Her face could not hide the confusion sweeping over it.

No one, not even her own family, had ever stood up for her that way.

Once in the kitchen, Caspar laid out the rodents on the counter before turning to her. He scanned her person, properly, for the first time since their unexpected embrace. Keziah found herself shuddering under his gaze. A sense of self-consciousness washed over her. Unable to meet his eyes, she stared at her feet in the pointed-toe slippers he'd lent her, though they were hardly enough distraction. She could feel the rest of her muscles tighten out of the knowing alone that he was watching.

Soon, his feet appeared in her field of vision. She smelled the musk lingering on his clothes before she felt his fingers beneath her chin. He guided her gaze upwards to meet his, taking her breath and words with him.

"Are you okay?" he asked, his voice soft but steady.

"I'm fine," she replied tersely, though, once again, his gentle touch caused her stomach to flip.

They lingered there, in the silence, her back pressed against the counter, and him, only a breath away. Neither of them seemed to have the strength to pull away, nor could they find the words to bridge the gap between them. It was as though they were standing on the opposing banks of a river, too close to ignore, yet too far to unite. Then, as if sensing her discomfort, Caspar dropped his hand.

She missed it almost as soon as he'd taken it from her,

though she questioned why such a thing would bother her in the first place. Caspar made for the other side of the kitchen, working in silence as he prepared dinner, but Keziah could not get over what had just transpired between them. What was this feeling of tightness in her chest? Had he seen her trembling under his scrutiny? Why did he stand up for her before, and why hadn't he said anything now? The only thing she knew for certain was that if she stayed here any longer, frustration would have her screaming.

"I am going to rinse off," she announced, practically galloping out of the house before she could hear his reply.

Once outside, she leaned up against the wall and took a deep breath. Her injured arm still ached, but somehow, that didn't bother her half as much as whatever had just happened between them.

One minute, he's defending me; the next, he can't even speak to me.

"What is wrong with me?" Keziah asked herself as she rested her head against the white clay. After another few deep breaths, things began to return to normal. Her chest began to open, her muscles eased, her heartbeat steadied, but her mind would not stop racing. She sighed. "We are not doing this…" she chastised herself as she lifted off the wall. "Rinse your face and compose yourself. You are the daughter of the chief, not some soppy peasant."

Keziah strode out back to the little trickle of a stream— their poor excuse for a washing station—and rinsed her hands clean of the rodent blood. She allowed the scent of lavender to saunter up her nostrils. Closing her eyes, she imagined she was home again, sat in the stone basin her father had made, soaking in crystalline water surrounded by petals as her *Tante* rinsed her hair. She hadn't realized how far she was from home until she opened her eyes again. Met with the sight of the harsh red clay and the trickle of water, Keziah's heart longed for a splash of green, a plush moss rug, even the sweet scent of petrichor.

I should really be heading home before they begin to worry…

In truth, only a small part of her wished to return home. The one that worried about her Tante and wished for her own bed. The rest of her relished in the respite from her father's prodding of marriage.

As far back as she could remember, he'd ignored her desires of wishing to practice with her powers, pushing her instead to focus on more "lady-like" pursuits. Things of which Keziah had absolutely no interest in learning.

Frustration bubbled up inside her. Keziah herself might have been stubborn, but her father was an immovable brute. Thinking of him now made her feel low, weak. Being around him was like being one of the marble statues of the imperial courthouses in the larger *Harri* towns, something to be seen but never heard. He treated her like she was a trophy to hand out, merely a prize to be won and not a winner of her own merit. Not even her voice, loud and imposing as it was, was enough to make him listen…

The thoughts were nauseating, suffocating. She felt she couldn't breathe beneath their weight. Her throat tightened. The pebbles at her feet vibrated. Anxiety took over.

Keziah reached her good hand up to her neck, searching for reprieve. In its search, her hand met silk. She ripped it from her neck and tossed it to the ground, fighting against the perceived suffocation. A low huff escaped her throat. As her breathing began to settle and her mind began to clear, she realized what she'd done.

The scarf Caspar had lent her to cover her hair lay before

her, crumpled in the dirt. His gesture of goodwill, cast aside like a fallen branch. A sour taste flooded her mouth. She took another few deep breaths as she stared at it, unease growing in the pit of her stomach. It reminded her that she was in the lands of their enemies, an outsider. Worse still, that even in the lands of their enemies, at least her opinions were given consideration.

Guilt riddled her body, replacing the previous frustrations. She bent down and retrieved the innocent scarf from the floor and hung it on a rock beside the stream—or trickle, more aptly named.

"Someone should really take care of this…" she said as she regarded it, placing her annoyance on the thing before her rather than the thing inside.

Then, a crazy idea came over her. She pressed her ear to the canyon wall that housed the little trickle. Closing her eyes to better hear, she searched the depths of stone for the source of the water. It took a moment to home in on the vibrations, but when she did, she was surprised to find pockets in the stone pulling from somewhere deeper. *An aquifer.*

Keziah pulled back, her eyes bouncing from the trickle to her still-damaged arm. She'd already proven to herself that she didn't *need* it to use her powers; though, out in the desert, she wasn't necessarily trying to be as precise with her targeting. This crazy idea of hers would require both precision and power.

She looked back at the house momentarily to make sure no one was watching.

I can fix this… she thought. *I know I can…*

At first, she tried to wiggle the fingers of her bad arm. A crippling shock of pain shot down from the gash to her fingertips. She sucked in a sharp intake of breath, clasping her hand over the wound. She knew she wouldn't be doing anything with that arm for a while, but the pain had not quelled the spark in her.

That spark—the one that usually got her into trouble—came with an intention so positively righteous it couldn't possibly fail. Could it?

She could fix it—she would fix it. She would prove to them all that she wasn't useless, that she wasn't here to cause trouble for anyone.

Keziah began simply by making soft swirling motions with her good wrist. The mud at the bottom of the stream obeyed, albeit defiantly, and slithered over to what Caspar had called a garden—and what looked more like the place where plants went to die. For now, she let it pile up to the side. Maybe when she got her full strength back, she'd set the garden straight, too.

"Good," she whispered to the earth as she admired the newly dug basin beneath the trickle. She figured it might be a good idea to lay some leaves at the bottom of it to prevent too much water from seeping back into the soil, but for now, this was a good start.

Earth was a stubborn element, but she was a stubborn girl. She supposed that's why she, like her father and his father and so on, had been born with such powers. To deal with such a stubborn element, it helped to be stubborn yourself.

"Now, for that sorry excuse for a stream…"

Despite the surprisingly constant trickle of water, the canyon face itself was made of well-baked desert clay and solid sandstone. If she hadn't been injured, she could've optimistically chopped it down in under an hour. The little pebble of doubt inside her had her considering whether she could make a dent in it at all. But Keziah would not let herself be deterred by it. Doubt, like a stone in one's pocket, weighed one down only so much as one let it. The more weight one attributed to it, the harder it would be to move. Or, at least, that's what her Tante always said.

Keziah looked back at the main house once more, conscious that she would have limited time before someone decided to check on her. Caspar was still mulling about the kitchen. If she meant to do something, she had to do it now.

There were pockets of air and water just behind the exterior wall. If she could just reach them, widen them a touch, more water would flow through the main spout. Keziah straightened her hand at her chest, sucked in a breath, and jabbed at the space before it with an opened palm. Her eyes widened as the small groove parted even more, releasing a slightly larger trickle into the basin.

That little pebble of doubt began to shrink. A smile grew at her lips, though she knew she could do better. Keziah widened her stance, pulled in a breath that reached down to her toes, and slammed a tight fist toward the rock. This time, the groove forked, connecting two inner pockets of the aquifer. The trickle merged into an easy flowing stream—a real stream.

The basin beneath steadily began to fill, but that still wasn't enough.

I can still do better, she thought, and readied herself for another strong hit.

"What do you think you're doing!" yelled Caspar's father from behind. Her time was up. As she'd imagined, he'd hobbled out of his room to check why she'd been missing so long. His harsh tone caught her off-guard mid-swing, and as a result, the undirected force of the blow collapsed one of the tunnels and blocked the stream entirely.

"Oh no, no, no…" Keziah whispered, wondering frantically how she could get the water flowing again before he realized. She tried flicking her wrist again to clear a bit of the debris, but to no avail. Her mind wasn't clear enough to move even a grain of sand.

Earth's stubbornness had won.

Caspar's father hobbled over to her, leaning mostly on his cane as he made his way past the garden. He stared briefly at the mound of mud before turning back to the rockfall that was once his shower.

"What have you done?!" His eyes bounced from the closed off groove in the canyon wall to the large hole of slowly vanishing water beneath it. When he finally glanced up at her, he frowned. Seeing her stance must have confirmed his grudge. "I knew you were bad news. You're *kanala*, aren't you?"

"Yes but—"

"I should've kicked you out the second I laid eyes on you," he growled, staring at her as though she were a muddied dog. "I can't believe Caspar brought you into the house. He knows better."

"I'm not an animal," she replied defiantly.

"You're worse than an animal. Your kind are the embodiment of destruction."

"I didn't mean to!" Keziah yelled in reply. "I was trying to fix it."

"It was never broken!" Caspar's father hissed. "That's the problem with you *kanala*, especially you *Harri kanala*. Everything is always broken! Everything needs fixing! Right?"

"I thought I could—"

"Everything must be touched by your Iturri-blessed hands!" he continued, unfazed by the redness flushing her cheeks or the offended look in her eyes.

Caspar, having heard his father's yelling, barrelled down the path from the house. "Father, stop." He planted himself firmly between Keziah and his father.

"Look at what she's done!" he raved once more. "I told you she was trouble. I told you the moment she set foot in the house."

Caspar glanced over at the mountain of rocks that blocked the water and sighed, but he turned back to his father with the same initial resolve. "Father, Keziah didn't mean to block the fountain. I'm sure it was an accident."

"Accident?! She's dangerous, Caspar. When are you going to open your eyes and see for yourself? *Her* kind are *all* dangerous."

"Father, listen to yourself. What would Mother say if she heard you speaking of another person that way?"

His father's face reddened, insult and injury taking up residence in his eyes. "Don't you ever bring up your mother to me again," he snarled, his voice echoing the howl of a wounded animal. "I want her gone before she wrecks anything else in this house."

He didn't wait for his son's reply before turning and hobbling back to the house. Keziah noticed his shoulders were hunched more than they had been when he was yelling at her. He'd insulted her more than anyone in her life, and yet, she felt a pang of guilt as she watched him up the path and into the house. For the first time, she saw him clearly. He was a lowly man whose hurt had become his identity, and she, for reasons unknown, was the embodiment of said hurt.

She turned back to Caspar, whose face could no more hide his disappointment than hers could hide her birth. Another wave of guilt flooded through her.

"I didn't mean to—"

But he held a hand up to silence her.

Normally, that wouldn't have stopped her. But Caspar was different. Everything about him was, which only made his actions hurt more.

"Leave it," he said with a heavy sigh. "I'll handle it. Just…" He paused, turning from her to the house and back again. "Maybe try and get some rest. We've had an eventful day, to say the least."

Guilt gurgled away in her stomach as she stared up at Caspar, finding it increasingly hard to meet his gaze. Her lips parted as if to speak, but her brain could not formulate the right words—or any words, for that matter. Keziah always had to have the last word, in every conversation, every argument. This time, she knew no words would suffice. She simply nodded and made her way back up the path, shoulders hanging unintentionally low like Caspar's father before her.

Maybe he was right.

Maybe she was nothing but trouble.

She snuck one last glance at Caspar over her shoulder, who stared defeatedly at the closed stream. She made up her mind in that instant to spare him the hassle and leave.

CHAPTER 6

KEZIAH HAD PLANNED TO WAIT PATIENTLY for nightfall to slip out unnoticed. She imagined that it would be easier to hide in darkness, though she wasn't quite sure how she would find her way home. The idea would come to her when she left the house, she was sure of it. But the seconds ticked by endlessly, and after just under an hour, she remembered that patience was never one of her strong suits.

Prodded on by the guilt and the embarrassment, Keziah lifted herself off the bed and wandered over to the window. The voices in her head had returned with a fury. She thought of her father and the trouble she'd be in, of her Tante, of her duties as the daughter of the Chief… And in the midst of the mental chaos, she thought of him, of the hunter who'd helped her where he could've left her for dead. She saw his face, confused, frustrated, but never cold. He'd been compassionate with her throughout, without reason and despite prejudice. He'd seen her, he'd held her, he'd protected her…

But why?

Between the strange interaction between her and Caspar, both in the desert and in the kitchen, and the encounter with his father in the garden, Keziah was at her wits' end. She knew she had to leave before she started to get any notions of things that could never be. She didn't belong here. She wasn't wanted here. Yet, her stomach curled at the thought of leaving.

He wants you here… whispered a little voice in the back of her mind.

"Quiet, you," she hissed. "It's not like I care either way…"

Keziah needed something to distract her, to pass the time; otherwise, she feared she'd go mad talking to herself. The stifling air of the hovel wasn't helping. She leaned out the window, staring out into the distance. Watching life pass by in the foreign land.

Little fires came to life in the village nearby—lanterns outside houses, along the paths, and in pits in the squares. People prepared for the dark—and to fend off the creatures of the night. Apparently, the fear of it was universal. It belonged to no one nation. At the end of the day, they were all only people, after all.

But the lights, welcoming as they seemed, did not help her situation. These streets were off limits. There, she would be prey to whomever decided she was an insult to their existence—or, as she quickly remembered, a threat. She would be seen as one of the prowling predators, yet she would be the one hunted. The streets were out of the question. Keziah needed somewhere where she would be otherwise untouchable.

As if by some twist of fate, a feather drifted down before her. Keziah turned her gaze upwards, facing the slight overhang of the roof. From the inside, it looked sturdy enough to support her additional weight. It might work to relieve her feelings of entrapment. Plus, if she stayed on the side closer to the canyon, no one would see her. She glanced back at the door. Somewhere beyond it, Caspar was fiddling about in the kitchen, preparing the day's catch. His father had already gone grumbling to his rooms. If she was quiet enough, neither would notice.

Keziah slung her legs out the window, balancing briefly on the sill as she manoeuvred the rest of her torso onto the lip of the roof. The challenge came with the fact that she could only use a single arm in the climb. Somehow, she managed to hoist herself up to a flattened landing. She breathed a sigh of relief as she rested her back against the inclined thatching.

From her own home, Keziah had never seen an open sunset. Her skies were covered by canopies, and even in the clearings, clouds prevented full appreciation of their vast expanse. The foliage of her own lands acted as a shelter from the outside world, something which had never bothered her until now.

This sky was different.

Expansive.

Here, the pinks and oranges of the setting sun looked to be stolen from the wildest flower bushes and fruit trees, the likes of which grew far from her own little slice of the forest. It reflected the vibrant burnt hues of the surrounding canyons. Unlike the baking midday sun, the feel of this light was different, warm without warning. It didn't scorch her skin as it had before. It didn't make her want to hide in the safety of the shade. It was cooler, softer, like a lullaby.

The desert was a strange place, a place of opposites. Keziah wondered how it could change so drastically within the span of only a few hours. Even more so, how these two extremes could coexist so harmoniously, as though it were necessity itself that would not see them part ways. As though they belonged together.

Keziah relished in the embrace of the cool desert evening. She found peace in the silence of it. The earlier stresses dissipated, leaving behind only a feeling of calm.

As the sun dipped behind the last stretch of desert and the cold of night swept in, Keziah noticed a strange set of lights appear in the sky. They reminded her of the flame-tipped arrows from her father's stories—the ones that featured the evil *Argia* and their dangerous control over fire.

Her eyes widened. Her heart began to race. She watched, alert to any sign of danger, but none came. Unlike the arrows in her father's stories, these strange balls of fire held their positions. Their glow strengthened with the fading sun, but they did not seem to be a threat.

After a while, she relented. Her muscles eased back into their resting state. Whatever those lights were, they did not seek to harm her. They were not the arrows of her father's stories.

Thinking back on them now, she realized those stories were the reason she'd been wary of Caspar all this time. The more time she spent with him, however, the more she began to question whether her father's stories had been embellished. She watched the twinkling lights above, charmed into a moment of introspection by their glow.

What would her father think of her now? Would he be worrying? And what kind of trouble was waiting for her when she got back?

Soon, even those questions disappeared, replaced by a resounding acceptance of her situation. Nothing would come of her worrying. There was nothing she could do now but wait.

As the full force of the night rolled in, more appeared. She gazed on, swinging her feet as they dangled over the lip of the roof, all but forgetting her plan to slip away.

"You act like you've never seen them before," Caspar called to her as he hoisted himself up to her perch.

Keziah suppressed a gasp. She'd been so lost in contemplation that she hadn't heard him approach. Her heart sank slightly. She wasn't escaping tonight.

"The stars," he said, waiting for her response. When none came, he inched himself closer, pointed skyward and added, "You have seen stars before, haven't you?"

Unlike before, Keziah didn't feel the urge to recoil in his presence. She found she wasn't afraid of him or annoyed by him at all. In fact, to her surprise, Caspar's presence was a welcome addition to her night.

Her eyes followed his finger upwards. *So, these are stars…* she thought.

Keziah had only ever heard stories of such things from the elders. She was never usually allowed to go out in the dark. By the time the sun had dipped below the canopy, she was in bed, like most all other women in the tribe. She'd heard of the occasional hunter who'd gotten lost and managed to find their way back thanks to the stars, but from the way people spoke about them, she'd thought the stars were a group of helpful people that guided lost travellers…

"I haven't," she admitted, turning back to them. "And is that…?" she asked, pointing to the thin sliver of silver in the sky. It looked like a semi-closed eye. She wondered if it watched them, the way they watched it.

"That is the moon…"

The moon. She'd never seen it so bright or vibrant. Usually, she was in bed before it was high enough to peek through the canopy. In her lands, the moon's rise signalled the hunt of the wolves—something she'd been protected from for as long as she could remember. Her eyes dipped to the ground below, searching for any signs of them now, but nothing about the red sandy landscapes suggested the presence of the prowling predators. Perhaps their soils were too flighty for the wolves' feet, too red for their grey hides.

"Do your people not pray to them?" Caspar asked.

"No," Keziah replied.

"Oh…"

"We pray to Iturri and to the earth, the source of our powers and the source of our strength," she added, realizing that he wasn't looking to mock her, rather make conversation. "These strange entities have no bearing over my life whatsoever."

Caspar chuckled. "It's curious how different we are… My people have always been taught to worship the sun and honour the stars. They are what brings light to our lives and fends off the dark."

"Your people are also known for burning down anything that doesn't outright have a heartbeat, and even those are only sacred if they come from your lands," Keziah said with more spite than she'd intended to. Unease crept into her stomach at hearing herself aloud. The words, she realized, felt tired and wrong coming from her lips, as though they belonged more to her father and her people than to her.

"That's not true," he countered, prompting her to

double down on her words.

"Your fires consume lands, making them unliveable for the creatures that once called them home."

Caspar furrowed his brow, offended at the accusation. "I don't know where you got that idea..."

Keziah turned her body to face him, borrowing her father's chastising gaze as she spoke. "Fire is dangerous. Everyone knows that."

"Don't you think we *Argia* would know that better than most?" he replied with a scowl.

Probably, she thought, but she wasn't about to back down now and seem foolish.

"Our people are taught to respect fire, taught what it means to burn and be burned," Caspar added when she didn't respond outright. "And contrary to what you believe, fire isn't something to be controlled. It has a life of its own. Once you set it free, it will do as it pleases... even, as you said, burn its way through entire landscapes. It's probably the most dangerous element, which is why *we* are careful with it, *kanala* or not."

"I still don't trust them..." she grumbled, though his words had landed. Maybe there was more to his side of the story than she'd been led to believe. But then, why would her father have lied? They weren't all good, she reminded herself, thinking back on the boys and their crude remarks from earlier. She used this as excuse enough to carve out a small exception for Caspar and Caspar alone.

Caspar chuckled softly, shaking his head as he contemplated her. "You're so stubborn."

"Now you're insulting me?"

"No. It's just... You say everything that's on your mind. No sifting through words. No trying to please. You're so…direct."

"I'm honest," she scoffed.

"It's different."

"You're different."

"It's refreshing," he whispered as he leaned back. He tucked his arms behind his head and rested his back on the thatching, probably hoping she wouldn't hear.

But she had. Keziah felt the heat of a blush creeping into her cheeks, thankfully hidden by the surrounding night. Even from his reclined position, Keziah was acutely aware of his gaze on her neck.

"I'm sorry for my father's behaviour earlier. He isn't usually such a grouch…" Caspar said before she'd got the chance to change the subject. When she looked at him again, bathed in the light of the moon, she realized how young he was. Though not much older than herself, he seemed to have gone through more lifetimes than she could fathom. She wondered how long he'd been charged with taking care of his father, wondered if he had any friends to speak of, and more so, how he could still smile in spite of his circumstances.

Keziah frowned, ashamed that she had so little to complain about comparatively, and having actively done so for the better part of her life. She tucked her knees into her chest and hugged her good arm around them. Her presence had only added to their misfortune, and even still, he couldn't act unkindly towards her.

"I didn't mean to cover it…" she whispered, knowing his father, as much as it pained her to admit, had been right. Her ego had gotten in the way—again. "I was only trying to make it wider."

"I figured."

"You figured?"

"I didn't take you for a saboteur," he grinned, which only made her feel worse.

"I don't want to cause a rift between you and your father..."

Caspar shot up, concern knotting his brows. "Is that what you think?"

"He clearly doesn't want me here. I don't belong—"

"Keziah, my father has a gripe with the world at large. Not just you."

"But you admit he doesn't like me."

Caspar sighed. "I think you remind him of her, my mother. You're bold, unapologetic, passionate. Those were all qualities he'd tout about her."

Keziah's blush deepened. She turned from him, hiding beneath the layers of ebony black hair. Even if he didn't mean them as compliments, they touched her heart. No one had ever referred to her in such glowing terms. It was almost a shame she couldn't stay here with him.

"I should probably leave..."

"I'd prefer you didn't," Caspar interjected quickly. "I mean..." he corrected himself. "Your arm still isn't healed. If you went back now, wouldn't that be seen as an act of war?"

"It would be disrespectful to stay against the wishes of an elder," she replied, though she was secretly grateful for his insistence that she stay.

"My father has a lot of inner turmoil to get over..." Caspar sighed. "It wasn't easy for him when my mother died. I was only a boy then, but even now, I remember the look on his face—the redness in his eyes, the burns on his hands and legs."

Keziah noticed his eyes had started to tear up mid-story. She wished to stop him, if only to save him from reliving the torment, but Caspar seemed insistent on sharing his story.

"The scent of ash wafted through the door behind him. But it wasn't nice like firewood. It smelled foul. I don't think I could explain it if I tried… Only later did I realize it was the scent of scorched bodies."

"I'm so sorry…" Keziah said softly.

"My mother didn't return home with him that day either. Somehow, she'd gotten herself caught in the middle of a blaze. Since then, my father hasn't trusted any of the *kanala*. And then, of course, being *Harri* doesn't help your case either…"

"I didn't realize…"

Caspar's smile was laced with melancholy. "How could you?"

Keziah thought of how Caspar's father's face had turned when he realized that she was *kanala*.

No wonder he hates me… she thought. Not only was she a nuisance to them for being *Harri*, but she was an even harsher reminder of all that he'd lost for being *kanala*. Now, she truly felt sorry for him. The old man, miserable as he was, carried a burden she couldn't even begin to imagine.

Keziah wished she could fix what she'd done. She wished to show him that not all *kanala* were the monsters he believed them to be… and not all *Harri* either. But from what Caspar had explained, Keziah realized his hatred ran much deeper. It was born of loss, of a grief that had been left to fester.

Those were the most stubborn and enduring roots of all.

"Tell me about your family," Caspar said, snapping her

out of introspection.

"What?"

"Come on," he added with a smile, though she could sense he needed to shift the focus from him and his grief. "You know my story. It's only fair."

"I mean, if you insist…"

"I do."

"Well, they're…" Keziah grumbled. "Difficult. Probably worse than your father."

"I doubt that," Caspar chuckled.

"No, really." Keziah turned to face him, unconsciously inching herself closer as she spoke. "My father is overbearing and overprotective. He wants to marry me off to some guy I've only met once and can already tell is self-obsessed and only interested in status."

Caspar bit down on a laugh. "That's quite a mouthful."

"My Tante rattles on to me about duty and how, when she was my age, she didn't have the luxury of arguing with her parents."

"I think that's all parents," Caspar replied, inching himself closer as well.

"And my brothers… They're… uptight? Annoying? And there are two of them!"

"That sounds…"

"Awful?"

"Nice. I've always wondered what it would be like to have siblings," Caspar admitted, though his voice softened. "I guess I should be thankful it's just me. I don't know how we would've lived with more mouths to feed…"

"Don't worry," Keziah replied softly. "You're not missing out on anything."

She hardly knew what possessed her to rest her good

hand over on Caspar's shoulder, only that she was grateful when he didn't immediately shrug it off. Then, when he rested his calloused hand over hers, she felt the traitorous blush return with renewed force. His hands were soothingly warm, even despite the chill that was beginning to settle around them. He squeezed her hand gently, the way he had when they'd returned, once again calling into question those impossible and improbable feelings.

"Thank you," he said. Keziah got the sense that he referred to more than just her gesture.

Unsure how to respond, she pulled her hand away and stared up at the night sky again. The balls of fire Caspar called "stars" seemed to be having a strange effect on her. Their bewitching glow robbed her of her impenetrable strength, of the wall she'd built around herself for her own protection. They made her *want* to share her stories with him, the poor *Argia* boy that had both shot her and saved her life. Maybe this was the friendship her brothers had so often urged her to find. But Keziah wasn't a fan of this new vulnerability; it felt too much like weakness, and she wasn't weak.

Curse you, stars, she thought as the night's chill wrapped around her shoulders, raising the hairs on her arms and legs.

"You're cold," Caspar remarked, staring at her now with a gentle glow in his eyes that matched the stars above. "We should head inside. Besides, the food is probably ready by now, and you must be starving."

Keziah couldn't decide whether it was the chill that sent shivers down her spine or the look in his eyes. She simply nodded, fearing that if she tried to speak now, the words could come out as incoherent babble. Caspar jumped down first and held his hands out.

"I'll catch you," he called.

"I can do it myself," she replied, afraid that if she let him catch her now, their tentative truce would turn into something more. And, pride or otherwise, that was something she could not permit.

She shimmied down the side of a fallen rain gutter with her good hand and dropped to the ground less gracefully than she'd hoped. As she wobbled on the balls of her feet, Caspar moved to steady her.

"You're so stubborn," he said with a frown. This time, she recognized it wasn't an insult, only a statement of his exasperation.

She righted herself without his help. "I'm independent."

Caspar sighed and shook his head but said nothing.

He led her into the kitchen, where the scent of charred meat welcomed them. His father had already served and tucked himself away in his room. Keziah found herself grateful that she wouldn't have to share a table with the man. Despite how she intended to fix things between them, she was glad not to have to avoid his harsh stares and insults as she ate.

The plates they used matched the teacup from earlier. A light glittering gold rimmed the chipped porcelain. All around the house, Keziah spied trinkets that seemed as if they might have once belonged to wealth, or even that Caspar and his father had once been able to afford a different life... Part of her wished to ask after the trinkets and niceties that now looked worn and in need of care, but she knew better than to prod at old wounds. Instead, she bit into the meat and moaned with delight.

The charred rodent wasn't nearly as bland as she'd expected it to be, and the accompanying bone marrow broth, though plain, warmed her like nothing had in a long time. She didn't even mind the stale bread, enjoying its taste when softened by the broth. Keziah wondered whether she enjoyed it because of her own hunger or because Caspar was a genuinely good cook. Either way, she would be remiss not to admit it was the best meal of her life.

When it was finally time for bed, Keziah lingered in the doorway, watching as Caspar laid out the blankets over the sofa, preparing it for sleep. She bit her lip, entranced at the way his shirt raised with his arms, exposing a toned lower back and dimples at the base of his spine. Despite the chill that sauntered through the open windows, Keziah found herself flushed with a new heat. Caspar fluffed his pillow before pulling his shirt over his head. Each time she'd seen him, he'd worn long sleeves and billowing tunics to ward off the desert sun. She hadn't realized that, beneath them, he'd hidden a muscled physique that slackened her jaw.

Keziah had never given much thought to how Caspar looked, but in the stillness of the night, she took pause. She studied the way his auburn locks drifted in the breeze, the tension in his muscled, sunburnt shoulders, she even found reason to admire his towering gait. In truth, he wasn't nearly as unattractive as she'd previously allowed herself to believe.

Caspar turned towards her, and having noticed her gaze, brandished an easy smile. "Goodnight, *kanala*," he called.

Keziah covered her mouth quickly and fled to the safety of the room. "Goodnight, hunter," she called back, hurrying to close the door.

What is happening to me? she wondered.

She was supposed to hate him. She'd been taught to hate all his kind, to fear them, and yet… Keziah waited with her heart in her throat. She leaned against the wall beside it, wondering if she had fled too soon.

From behind the door, she heard Caspar's footsteps draw near before stopping. Had he planted himself on the other side? Keziah leaned her head in near and held her breath. She could hear Caspar's heavy breath behind the door. What would she do if he knocked? Would she pretend to be sleeping? Would she let him in? The seconds ticked by eternally. She couldn't get involved, especially not as she'd planned to leave that night when he was sleeping.

Finally, she heard a sigh and Caspar's voice beyond the door. "Sleep well," he called. She listened out for his fading footsteps as he moved back to the sofa, disappointment settling in the pit of her stomach.

"And you…" she whispered to the closed door, too awake to sleep.

❧ CHAPTER 7 ❧

CASPAR WAITED AT THE DOOR; HAND READY but afraid to knock. He wasn't ready to let Keziah go just yet. Not after such an eventful day. And, as if his life hadn't been sufficiently altered by her presence, their conversation on the roof had left his mind reeling.

Though brief, those moments under the stars had given him much to think about. Caspar had never been one to speak so openly about his situation to anyone. Yet, this strange *Harri* girl had coaxed it out of him with nothing more than a glance. She'd turned his head upside down in under a day and left him unable to reconcile the strange feelings growing in his chest.

His hand trembled at the edge of the door, as if wanting to force itself down upon the wood. Perhaps he was merely tired. The day's events had been more up and down than the canyons themselves. He wondered if he hadn't only been spurred on by the charming stillness of the cold desert night and the promise of a hot meal. Perhaps if he acted on whatever he felt in that moment he would regret it in the morning. After all, there was no future to be had between them. They were too different.

Caspar relented to the intrusive thought, convincing himself that they had only been moments after all. Moments like any others that would vanish with the morning sun.

Moments that hardly felt real, let alone his.

"Sleep well," he whispered through the wood as his fist dropped to his side. Caspar begrudgingly reminded himself that, despite whatever feelings he was beginning to harbour, Keziah was not from these lands, nor was she here to stay. Cozying up to her would do him no good when she decided it was time to leave—as he knew she would.

This isn't real, he reminded himself. *Real will be the day she leaves. We were never meant to meet in the first place...*

In spite of these thoughts, Caspar found himself turning over the idea of her *not* leaving in his head. When he'd taken her in the day before, he hadn't expected to take pleasure in her company, let alone find himself endeared to her. She was an enigma of a woman, and though he'd been the one to save her, a small part of him felt like he was the one being saved. He found himself staring at the cracks in the ceiling for over an hour before his eyes finally drifted closed. In his dreams, he saw only her.

* * *

As the dawn rays slowly filtered in through the windows, Caspar was already awake, preparing a fresh batch of mint tea for the household. He slipped out as it was steeping, a parcel of cutlets under his arm to trade with the baker for a cinnamon loaf. He was glad to have something to be able to trade for the small luxury. He knew both his father and Keziah would appreciate the surprise. Caspar was in a better mood that morning than he had been in years—even the baker remarked on the gleam in his smile.

When Caspar returned home, he set out to prepare the teacups and plates, finding himself humming one of the campfire tunes his mother used to sing to him. He took a cup of steaming hot tea with him as he made for Keziah's door. His hand hovered before it, poised to knock, as he wondered if she was already awake or if he'd wake her.

"She's not there," his father said, a scowl lining his face as he poured himself a cup.

"What are you talking about?"

"Your…whatever she is. She's not there."

Caspar opened the door frantically, almost dropping the cup as he stared at the empty bed. "What did you do to her?" he growled at his father.

"You need to stop acting like this is okay. It's not. If people find out—"

"Father, Keziah is a person. I'd appreciate it if you stopped regarding her otherwise," Caspar said, resting the cup on the table so he wouldn't break it between his trembling hands.

"She's not like us. She needs to go back where she belongs, and you need to forget you ever met her."

"She's nothing like the people from your stories. She's different."

"Don't kid yourself, boy," his father spat. "They're all the same. She's got it in her blood."

"Give it a rest, Father!" Caspar scoffed. He was tired of his father's stubbornness. His father didn't know Keziah like he did. She wasn't the reason for his misery. She was as much a victim of circumstance as any of them. "I don't see what you have against her."

His father took a step back. "I will not see you get hurt…" he replied, his voice low.

"Father, none of it is your concern," Caspar growled as he snatched his hunting gear from the small table in the sitting room. "And you can relax. There is nothing going on between me and Keziah. But know this: if there *was*, it would *still* be none of your concern."

His father's eyes narrowed as they fixed on him. "You're not falling in love with her, are you?"

Love. That one, seemingly innocent word rippled through him, wreaking havoc on his heart. His breath caught in his throat. The memory of last night, of her hand on his shoulder, of her eyes sparkling in the moonlight, it all came rushing back. *Is this…love?* He knew he had to do something to keep his father off his back. Caspar closed his eyes, fighting against the tightness in his chest.

He exhaled deeply, strapping on his bow and quiver as he marched towards the door.

"As I said, it's none of your concern." He didn't know what he was or wasn't beginning to feel for her, only that he'd be damned if he let something happen to her out there. "I don't have time for one of your lectures. I am going to find her."

"No need."

"Stop! Stop it now," Caspar demanded. "She made one mistake, and only because she was trying to help. I'm sick of hearing you complain about a woman of whom you know absolutely nothing."

"Son, you should know—"

"No, Father, you should know that the reason we met was because *I* was out in *their* woods trying to find us food, and she was there because her people won't let her practice her powers. I shot her by accident and almost killed her because of your nagging voice in my head." Caspar ignored his father's attempts at interruption. "Did you also know, her family is trying to lock her into an arranged marriage with a man who cares not for her as a person and will probably cage her like all the rest?" His father frowned. "Keziah has enough on her plate without you constantly moaning about her presence or treating her like some wild animal."

His father sighed. "She's not out there. She's in the garden," he said as he plucked a cinnamon roll from the kitchen and hobbled back to his room. "Make sure she doesn't destroy anything else trying to fix something that wasn't broken…"

Caspar dropped his weapons and barrelled towards the back garden, breathing a sigh of relief as he spied her fighting with a tangle of dried branches. He hadn't realised how fast his heart was racing until now, feeling its pulse heavy in his chest as he watched her from the edge of the dug-out patch of fresh soil.

Keziah had managed to tie her raven-coloured locks up with a scarf, which she wiped a sweaty arm on as she worked. Something about the way the scorching morning sun hit her skin made it look as though she were glowing, as though she were a singular sprout of life in their desert of a garden. Caspar watched, mouth agape, as she tended to the harsh soils.

Her movements were gracefully precise. Each jab of her hand, each stomp of her foot, each flick of her wrist had a purpose. The earth bent to her whims. Caspar could do nothing but watch on in awe. She looked up from her work and contemplated him with a curious tilt of her neck.

"Has something bitten you?" she called out.

"What?"

"One of those viper things you were afraid of," she clarified. "Your eyes are wide like a baby moss-elk."

Caspar blinked incredulously. "I thought you'd left."

"Your garden is in a terrible state," she said, ignoring his question.

Caspar thought he caught a glimpse of a blush creeping into her cheeks, but it might also have been the heat. His heart steadied as he passed a glance around the plot of dried earth and untended thorns.

"I haven't had time to look after it since…" he trailed off, the memory of his mother returning.

"It'll take a miracle to get anything growing here again," she said, changing the subject before the sadness set in. "Luckily for you, I am one," she added, her blasé tone hinting at another verbal sparring match.

Caspar grinned as he collected a mattock that hung on the exterior of the house and slung it over his shoulder. "You're definitely not ordinary, I'll give you that," he said as he returned to her side.

"We cannot all be hunters who are incapable of hunting," she mused.

"Be careful, *kanala*, I wouldn't insult the one tending to your injuries," Caspar replied as he drew closer to her, a coquettish smirk growing on his face.

"Clearly, hunter, the one tending to my injuries has not yet learned that I back away from nothing," she countered, closing the gap between them as she stared up into his eyes.

"Is that so?"

"I am a fearless warrior who can handle anything…"

"Hmm…" Caspar rested the mattock on the floor and

aimed his hands at her sides.

"What are you—" she began, but her words were cut short, replaced by laughter as he tickled her relentlessly. "Stop," she giggled as she tried to push off of him.

Suddenly, a whip of small pebbles sent him tumbling to the ground. Caspar was unharmed but decided to play a cheeky trick on Keziah. He remained still, as though he'd been knocked out by a larger stone. As he expected, she dropped to the ground at his side, terrified that she might have hurt him.

"Oh no! I didn't mean—I'm so sorry..." she stuttered.

When he couldn't bear the sound of her tortured voice any longer, he reached up and hugged her in close before pinning her to the ground in an otherwise compromising position, dirtying her as she had him. Keziah screamed in delight, and Caspar got to relish in that beautiful smile of hers once more.

"You scoundrel!"

"I thought you said you could handle anything?" he said with a smirk.

"Maybe I was going easy on you," she argued.

"Maybe your defence needs work," he countered.

The pair of them locked eyes in a staring match that, to Caspar, felt both eternal and over all too soon. Keziah bit her lip, a smile curled at the sides of her mouth. Caspar could feel his heart racing again. The sound of it pounded loudly in his ears. He worried Keziah might hear it. A strange heat made its way from his chest to his stomach and further down, but before anything happened, Keziah tossed him backwards with another whiplash of dust.

She rose to her feet, dusted off her tunic, and smiled over him. "My attack, however, works just fine," she said as she extended her good hand for him to take. "Now, hunter, uproot your feet and dig along the lines I've traced. If we start now, we might be able to get the soil turned and all the roots and stones out before midday. I have a feeling by that time, this sun will be unforgiving at best."

Caspar bit down on his growing smile. "Yes, ma'am." He reached down, collected the mattock, and began breaking up the clay following the lines she'd already made in the ground. Meanwhile, Keziah started on the pebbles, moving them in sweeps into a pile where they could be used later. Out of the corner of his eye, Caspar watched as she worked, commanding the stones into something resembling a barrier around the garden.

Whatever vision she had for the space was exceptionally well thought out—much better than anything he could've thought up on his own. It was easy to see she knew her way around the earth, something she and his mother had in common, from what little he remembered of her. In her moves and motives, Caspar saw reverence, respect, and understanding that he could scarcely comprehend. It was hard not to watch on in awe.

Caspar had never met anyone like her, and not because she had been born to a different nation. He'd never met anyone so unashamedly herself, so unafraid to stand out or challenge him. If the rest of the people in his life were torch flames, Keziah was a bonfire.

Is this...love? The thought reappeared in his mind, both a reminder and a warning. They were from two different worlds, too far to be bridged. Yet, each smile of hers was a stone, paving the way to a union, a friendship, a something more...

They spent the rest of the morning working and joking

under the soft heat of the early sun. Caspar knew they had little less than an hour before that same heat would force them into the shade. But he had a plan. There was a place nearby that he'd been fond of as a boy that he wished to show her. A "thank you" for everything she'd done on the garden—and on him.

"I've created furrows along the crop rows. We can line them with pebbles to keep the water from evaporating. Over there," she said, pointing to one of the flatter canyon walls, "I want to create a catchment system. I think I should be able to create small channels that flow from there to beneath the plants so that they have a relatively steady supply of water…"

"You know you don't have to do any of this, right?" he interrupted.

Keziah tilted her head at him. "What do you mean?"

"This isn't your home. You don't owe us anything," he replied, and for a split second, he thought he'd spied the makings of a frown on her face.

"Are you saying you don't want my help?"

"No…" Caspar blushed. "That's not it. Not at all."

"Then what?" she prodded, her eyes narrowing on him.

Caspar swallowed hard on the ball forming in his throat. "Why?"

"Why does it matter?" she growled in response.

Caspar wished he could've taken the question back almost as soon as he'd spoken it. No good would come from it. What had he even hoped to hear in response?

That she abhorred the sight of the garden?

That she took pity on him for his impoverished circumstances?

That she was simply repaying kindness before

abandoning him?

Or, even more laughable, that, in spite of it all, she was falling in love?

A poor hunter and the daughter of a chief... He turned the ridiculous thought over in his mind, finding no solace or relief. *Regardless of our nations, it would never work.*

As if sensing his dilemma, Keziah frowned fully. She rested her good hand over the bandage on her other arm and turned from him, her shoulders hanging lower than before.

"I need a drink..." she said disappointedly.

"I'll get—"

"No. It's fine." She avoided his gaze as she made her way back up to the house.

With each step she took, he felt the makings of a rift he'd never intended to create. Guilt gnawed at his insides. One word was all it had taken to remind him that they could never be. And yet, a little part of his heart kept nagging at him.

What have I done?

Suddenly, a flash of white caught his eye. Caspar focused his attention beyond the blocky walls of their house, where a figure was disappearing down the road. He frowned. Had someone seen her? They hadn't done a great job of hiding, but Caspar hadn't known anyone to wander down this far. They lived on the edge of the town. Anyone who had come this far would have reasons to do so.

Caspar strode up to the edge of their property and peered over their wall. Whomever it was had gone, and whatever they'd seen was a mystery. They would have to be more careful from now on. He had no idea how the people of his town would react to Keziah's presence, but he highly doubted that it would be a celebration, especially if they found out that she was *kanala*.

❧ CHAPTER 8 ❧

KEZIAH DRAGGED HER FEET AS SHE MADE her way back up to the house. She'd been working tirelessly since dawn, having snuck past Caspar in the sitting room to be able to surprise him with her efforts. And yet, Caspar had looked almost suspicious of her work. His question had injured her almost as much as his arrow. Could he not see that she'd done it for him?

She pressed a hand to the door, waiting at the precipice. Beneath her, subtle vibrations in the ground told her that Caspar's father was asleep and snoring. *Better,* she thought, peeking through the ajar door to ensure his father was nowhere in sight. Caspar's question had damaged her ego enough. She didn't think she could take another blow.

Caspar's father had fallen asleep in the sitting room. Keziah had intended to simply sneak past him and into the kitchen, but something caught her eye. Upon closer inspection, she realized there was something pinned between his arm and his chest. She tiptoed over to him as quietly as she could, though she was admittedly poor at dulling the heaviness of her steps. Luckily, his father was a heavy sleeper.

Keziah peered over his shoulder and down at the flimsy parchment. It was a sketch of a woman with long black hair and features that looked closer to her own than to those of the *Argia*.

How strange, she thought. For someone who was such a staunch critic of her, Keziah wondered what he was doing with such a picture. But she knew better than to ask anything of him.

She cast the thought aside, slipped into the kitchen and poured herself a cup of cold tea. From the kitchen window, she contemplated their work in the garden. There was still more to do, but it was coming along nicely.

If only her own father could see the kind of work she could do with her powers, he might not be so against her using them. There was so much good to be done with them that didn't include waging wars with other tribes in the name of "keeping peace," as he so often put it. The strength Iturri had blessed her with didn't need to be used for violence. If she could only show him, maybe he would understand.

Even Caspar, a man of their enemies, seemed to have changed his tune quickly enough. He didn't seem afraid of her anymore, though he may still hold reservations. If he as a rival could see the good in her powers, surely her father could see reason.

Caspar's father grumbled. Keziah peeked over at him to ensure he was still sleeping. Their fathers came from the same generation. One that held fast to traditions and hatreds without question. She frowned as she contemplated him. As much as it pained her pride to admit, considering the difference in their circumstances, they were more alike than they realized.

Keziah tiptoed past him again and made her way back into the garden, breath hitching in her chest as she caught sight of Caspar once more.

He hadn't noticed her return; lost in the rhythm of the work she'd left him with. The mattock glinted in the sun high above his head. His auburn locks shone like cords of brass. Beads of sweat clung to his person, glittering the sunlight. She'd frozen in place as she watched him, caught in a moment of admiration. He brought the tool down hard on the packed soil, the muscles in his back rippling through the move—he was shirtless.

She watched in awe, her mouth agape. Her heart quivered—*the traitor.*

Keziah knew she shouldn't be attracted to him. He looked nothing like the men of her tribe, nothing like the men her father had tried to force her into a life with. He was thinner, his muscles were fine, belonging to the eagle rather than the fattened bull. His skin was the colour of the lifeless desert sands—taupe and shallow in comparison to the richness of that of her own people. His shoulders were not heavy enough to carry an ox. His hands were not swollen and broad. This was not the image of beauty her lands had described. Yet, she found she could not look away. She saw in him something new, something exciting, something so alive it clawed at life itself. Her eyes widened. Heat pooled in her stomach.

For the first time, she saw a predator.

And though a predator, she reminded herself, he was still soft inside. Soft enough to hold her close in the face of danger, to comfort her against shame. He was an eagle with the heart of a dove.

As if sensing her stare, Caspar turned, the mattock high above his head. Their eyes met. For a long time, neither made a sound. They stared at each other, as if waiting to see who would back down first. In the end, Caspar relented.

He tossed the mattock to the floor with a soft thud and strode up to her. Keziah felt her heart beating viciously in her chest, as though it were ready to leap into his arms. His steps unknowingly fell in tune with the drumbeat of her heart.

Thump, one step. *Thump*, two step. *Thump*, three step…

She held her breath as he neared.

Thump, thump, th—

He was no more than a breath in front of her. She looked up at him, forcing her mouth to speak, though her mind had lost all proper sense.

She blinked.

He smirked.

"You're not finished, hunter," she whispered finally.

"It's time for a break, *kanala*," he replied, a knowing grin spreading across his face.

Keziah could have melted then and there…

Caspar clearly had a different version of melting in mind.

* * *

The scorching afternoon sun sapped the world of colour. It sat high in the sky above them, bearing down like an emperor in his throne upon the weary. The lands below were thirsty; ripples of heat rose in the distance. Even the winds begged for reprieve.

Keziah had almost wished they'd stayed in the house and out of the heat. Caspar had offered her new robes and slippers—billowing layers of white cotton and gemstone adorned slippers—before they departed, to protect her from the desert sun. With the splashes of colour on the slippers and headscarf, Keziah was beginning not to mind the plain white of the fabrics. Once again, she questioned where Caspar, given his circumstances, had gotten slippers that looked to be worth much more than his house, but she knew better than to ask after painful answers.

They walked for what felt like just under an hour, much farther than the cave she'd located the previous day. Concern crept into her heart with each sand dune they passed, but Caspar reassured her the surprise would be well worth the wait.

Soon, they came to the mouth of a large cave. The air flowing through it was cool and damp—the kind that reminded her of home. A strange roar came from within, one she'd never heard before. It came growling in waves, too frequent to be a creature, though Keziah had a hard time picturing what else it could be. It was as though the rock itself was breathing.

Keziah halted at the precipice, focusing her energy on the ground beneath her. The vibrations came in, constant and haphazard. What was this strange cave?

"Is everything okay?" Caspar asked, noticing her contemplative pause.

"I thought you were afraid of caves," Keziah said as she raised a brow at him.

"This one is different," he replied, a mischievous smile growing at his lips. "Do you trust me?" he asked as he extended his hand towards her.

Keziah looked from the mouth of the cave to that eager smile of his. She hesitated for only a second. If the notoriously cautious Caspar was not afraid, she figured she had little reason to be either. Still, she wished she knew what beast lay at the other end of the cave.

She nodded, taking hold of his outstretched hand as she followed him into the darkness.

Do you trust me? She played his words over in her head, a small frown forming at the edge of her lips. After all they'd been through, and despite her attempts against it, she found there was already a seedling of trust in her heart. It wasn't all encompassing. Not yet. But she feared that each interaction might water it. And then, when it was inevitably time to go, what would become of it?

The deeper they got into the tunnel, the louder the roaring became. Keziah's steps unwittingly grew closer and closer to Caspar's until, like with the boys at the edge of the town, she was practically under him. He kept his gaze forward, though she could see a smile playing at the edge of his lips. This, paired with the warmth of his body and his lavender-infused musk, made her heart flutter. Heat prickled in her cheeks. Thankfully, the dark would keep it hidden.

At the end of the tunnel, Keziah spied a soft blue light. The crashing sound faded, as they were no longer in the line of the echo. The tunnel itself gave way to a hideaway—a cove filled with pebbles, sand, and a pool of glowing, churning water. The damp cave walls reflected speckles of sunlight from high above. The coolness of the place was a far cry from the scorching heat from whence they'd come.

Keziah's jaw slackened as she regarded the natural beauty. She'd never seen anything like it. It was something out of a story.

"What is this place?" she asked, releasing Caspar's hand as he wandered closer to the edge than she was comfortable.

Curious, she slipped out of the shoes and placed her bare feet on the pebbled shore. A soft sigh escaped her lips as she relished in the feel of the cool pebbles beneath her feet, a welcome reprieve from the outer heat.

"A secret beach," Caspar replied as he began stripping off his shirt. "I figured we could use something to cool us down after all that hard work."

"Oh…" she mumbled as she watched the waves wash upon the pebbled shore. The shifting earth beneath her feet gave her little confidence. She was a far cry from the soils and deep-seated rocks she'd grown used to, and farther still from any sort of comfort she'd established in her limited surroundings.

Keziah inched closer to where the pebbles gave way to sand. She scrunched her toes in it as the low grumble of the waves crept up to her feet. Keziah jumped; the water was colder than she'd imagined.

Judging by the roar, she figured the water flowed through a chasm that went down for miles before spewing its guts out into what she imagined was some far-flung ocean. Her eyes fixated on the waves that pulled everything out to the centre of the cave. They came in calm and steady pulses, but that didn't make them any less threatening.

The beach was beautiful, there was no doubt about that, but also terrifying. Here, the pebbles shifted too much for her to find her footing. The vibrations created by the waves made it impossible for her to sense anything with any clarity. Usually, when she worked with the earth, she could distinguish between the few stones and the dirt. Here, it was all a confusing mess of stones, and unmovable sands. Not only was it her first time on a beach, but also without her powers.

Keziah had only ever heard about beaches and oceans in tales from the elders. Her little patch of the forest was entirely landlocked. She'd seen ponds and lakes, even the occasional waterfall. But all of those were contained. They didn't roar the way this place did. They didn't smell salty and briny in a way that made her nose hairs curl. They didn't threaten to swallow her and spit her out far from solid ground—or worse, into a watery grave.

This was new territory. Unfamiliar in the worst of ways. She gulped as she took another tentative step towards the shore. The barrage of vibrations beneath her feet from the retreating wake rattled her soul. Earth alone never moved this much. Water was a crafty and disorienting element.

"Are you okay?" Caspar asked, snapping her out of her fear-ridden trance. "You're not shy now, are you?"

It's just a bath, Keziah told herself. *You take baths all the time.*

"Not even close," she replied. In a single swoop of her good arm, she stripped off her outer robe, attempting to distract him from the hesitancy creeping into her eyes. Caspar in turn removed his pants, beginning a game in which they removed layer after layer until the only thing covering her body was the small swathe of cloth that bandaged her wound. By then, they were both bare-skinned and entirely exposed.

The game played out the way she'd intended. It seemed to distract Caspar enough from the way her mood had shifted, but not even his naked form could quell the fears ringing out in her head.

It's just a little water, she reminded herself.

A little water that happens to move on its own and might swallow me whole.

She inched closer to it hesitantly as the back and forth in her head continued.

It's a bath...

...a bath that drops off the edge of the world if I move too deep...

Somewhere behind her, she heard Caspar's voice prattling on about something that she would pretend to remember later. Right now, the conversation in her head took centre stage.

Stop it, Keziah. Your father didn't raise you to fear...

He also didn't teach you to swim...

"Keziah, I—" Caspar began, but before he could get another word out, she raced into the shallow waters.

They were even colder than she'd expected, though the shock to her system helped her forget her nerves. Keziah let out the heavy huff that had risen with the goosebumps across her skin. There was a slight tug at her from the far end of the cave. It was a soft current, but not one so terrible that it would whisk her away unwittingly. Nothing so strong that she couldn't keep herself upright and near the shore, but something to be mindful of further out—not that she would get that far.

Just like a bath...

Keziah took deep breaths, allowing herself to relax as she closed her eyes and immersed herself fully. As she dunked her head beneath the saltwater, she imagined it was simply one of the shallow rock pools of her home that she'd bathed in under heavy clouds of lavender soaps.

The wound beneath the bandage on her arm began to sting. The sensation was uncomfortable, but not unbearable. The salt in the water gnawed at her still-healing skin in a way that reminded her of the salve Caspar had placed on it after the initial injury. A few seconds in and the stinging became a soothing throb that, once acknowledged, became an afterthought.

When she surfaced, she found the cold of the water less biting, and the tug of the current less threatening. Keziah planted her feet firmly into the gravelly sand beneath her until she touched the basal layer of rock. She found comfort, little as it may have been, in the stability of it.

Perhaps it wasn't as bad as she'd thought.

Her inky black hair pooled around her as she rose, glistening like slick oil on the surface of the water. She twirled around in the crystalline water, laughing like a child, relishing in this curious new experience. She spun, once, twice. None of the baths she'd been in had been this vast. There was a certain freedom to this beach that tugged on her heart. The juxtaposition between her home and this empty, cavernous shore reminded her of just how trapped she'd felt in her village. And then, amidst her moment of introspection, their eyes met.

Keziah's heart froze.

Caspar made no effort to hide his burning stare.

As she watched him, Keziah felt a blush creeping into her cheeks. Like she'd told him, she'd never been shy of the naked form. However, ever since the previous night, she'd grown bashful around him. She noticed a fluttering in her stomach every time she thought of sharing moments with him—naked or otherwise. It was strange to think the flimsy clothes he'd lent her had offered any sort of protection. But, standing before each other, fully exposed, she realized they had been yet another wall she'd erected between them for protection.

Caspar exposed was everything she'd imagined and more. She knew his form would haunt her dreams, and she would be forevermore helpless to stop it. Keziah lowered herself deeper into the water, hiding her fluster just below the surface, but making sure her hesitant feet still felt some semblance of ground beneath them.

Sparing not another moment's hesitation, Caspar dove in after her. His graceful dive left only a small splash on the surface as he glided beneath the waves.

Keziah found herself twisting to find where he had gotten to, but he was nowhere to be seen. She waited to hear him resurface for air, but the sounds of the small waves echoed too loud to hear anything else.

The seconds ticked by. Keziah grew restless. She knew his dive would've taken him from the clearer parts of the water to the darker depths, but she still expected him to have surfaced already.

"Caspar?" she called out to the depths where the water flooded back out into the ocean. In her mind, her voice barely sounded over the roaring waves. The only response she received was the soft gliding of sand and pebbles beneath the retreating wake. Keziah took a tentative step deeper into the water, casting her eyes about in search of a bright pop of auburn hair or paler skin, but she found nothing.

Just as she was about to call out again, she felt arms swoop her up and out of the water from behind. Pressed against something hard, Keziah squirmed. It took her a moment before she managed to wriggle around, meeting in that moment Caspar's coquettish grin.

"You were scared," he smirked as he whipped his hair out of his eyes.

"I was not!" The vicious beat of her heart said otherwise.

"I didn't think you'd miss me that much," he added,

holding her a little tighter.

"I did not," she managed to hiss before Caspar dunked her into the water without warning.

As she resurfaced in his arms, he raised an eyebrow and said, "It's not good to lie."

"It wasn't a—" she began, before he plunged her once more unceremoniously into the water.

"Try again," he said, the grin growing wider as he stared into her eyes.

"I—" was all she managed this time before dipping beneath the water. This time, on the way back up, she squirmed just enough in his arms to allow her to free her good arm, hoist herself up onto his head and submerge him. Caspar resurfaced laughing as he wiped the soaking strands of auburn hair from his eyes. "Serves you right," Keziah hissed as she splashed him again.

And it did. He had no idea the fear that had flooded through her in those brief seconds. If something had happened to him, she wouldn't have been able to save him. She, like all the other rocks she knew, was unable to swim. Caspar, on the other hand, seemed surprisingly agile in the water. Agile enough for the both of them, she hoped.

But Caspar did not linger on the fear in her eyes. He brandished a warm smile up at her, as if to say she had no need for whatever fears resided in her.

"Funny, I thought I put out all the fire you had in you…" he replied as he gazed up at her. The twinkle in his eye sparked a challenge in her, one that helped the anxiety subside.

"Never," she said, crossing her arms over her chest. The corner of her lips lifted. Some of her usual fierceness resurfaced alongside him. Keziah doubted he realised how much she needed this, the chance to stand up for herself after a moment of fear. She latched onto that fleeting feeling of strength, using it as an anchor for the rest of her emotions.

"Never? Strong word," he said with a smirk.

"Strong words from a strong girl."

"I didn't say otherwise." His voice lowered. "I half expected you to snarl at the association."

"What, the fire?" She grinned, taking a tentative step closer. "What has a little fire got on me?" Staring into his eyes, Keziah found the echoing sounds of the waves crashing against the cavern walls and the dragging of the wake on the shore began to fade.

All of a sudden, she was intimately aware of the space between them and the way Caspar began to close it. The moment they shared no longer seemed to belong to friends.

"Not a very *Harri* response…" Caspar growled teasingly. The sound may have come out as nothing more than a whisper, but to her ears, his voice was the loudest thing around. His movements were slow, tentative, as though he feared she were as ephemeral as the echoes around them. His rugged hands wrapped around her waist, taking their time against the soft push of the waves. His fingers left streaks of fire across her skin as they glided over her ribcage and down to the base of her spine. "Sounds more *Argia* than anything."

"Careful, hunter, I might just burn you," she replied, fighting against the shivers that wanted to appear beneath his fingers. Possessed by the pounding in her chest, she inched closer as well.

"Well, *kanala*, I'm beginning to think you might be right."

Keziah stood in her power, watching as he took the lead. The same feelings from the previous night had resurfaced. This time, however, she was not going to flee.

Something in Caspar had changed as well. No longer did he seem like the boy who hid his blush after seeing her exposed body. Now, he stared up at her in all her glory, his eyes scanning her person dotingly. It was the same look she'd worn as she'd gazed upon the stars the previous night.

No one had ever looked at her that way.

Despite the idea of him she'd built up in her head, her reservations, the differences between them, she found she could no longer deny their similarities. Nor could she deny the feelings she'd slowly developed for him.

Keziah felt him tense against her, as if fearing what were to come next. This time, a new set of nerves rushed through her body, but these ones were steeped in anticipation. She'd stopped herself from going any further with him the other night, but she'd had the door to help. This time, there was no door, no separate room. This time, there was only the here and now, and the pull between their two bodies in the shifting waves.

Would she go through with it?

Could she?

The waves caught glints of sunlight from up high and reflected them back into Caspar's eyes. Their amber colouring glowed as bright as the red rocks of the canyons of his homeland. He was all fire, but remembering the vivid hues of the desertscape, she realised there was a little earth in him as well.

Keziah ran her fingers tentatively through his dripping auburn locks. She was done fighting against whatever attraction had surfaced between them, especially now as his hands pulled her down on top of him, pressing her against his torso. She followed his cues as he guided her body to straddle his lap. His rugged hands rode up the sides of her hips and trailed behind her back.

With eyes locked on each other, the rest of the world's cues went mute. Time had stopped for them, encasing them in their wildest fantasies. His breath, her heartbeat—the only sounds ringing in her ears. It all happened so agonizingly slow for her, but she knew she would recall the moment in time with its true brevity.

With a knowing smile, she brought her face intimately close to his, letting her next words fall directly onto his lips.

"I'm always right," she replied with nothing more than a whisper.

In an instant, whatever semblance of cool Caspar had played at throughout their time together vanished. His lips were on hers faster than a twig rabbit could pound its foot. Their bodies collided. He gripped her as a lover might—as she'd always hoped a lover would. His fingers found themselves tangled in her hair as her legs wrapped around his waist. They leaned into each other. The fervent frenzy silenced all thoughts, quelled all fears. Keziah was suddenly so overrun with passion that she'd hardly noticed they'd drifted into deeper waters…

♦ CHAPTER 9 ♦

CASPAR HELD ONTO HER BODY TIGHTER than he'd ever held anything in his life. Now that he'd finally given in, gotten her in his grasp, he couldn't bear the thought of losing her. He lost track of everything but the soft feel of her skin in his hands, the plumpness of her lips against his, and slightest of spine-tingling moans that she let out as his fingers traced down her back. His mind, alongside his body, had willingly surrendered to the senselessness of passion.

He shifted along the seabed with the tides, ignoring their increasing ferocity as the currents dragged them further into the depths. He hardly noticed the way they'd slipped away from the shore until he found himself sliding one foot off the jagged edge of the rocky sea floor and into the cavernous void.

"Ouch!" he called out from beneath her, feeling the sharp rocks slice cleanly through the sole of his foot, but the sound was quickly muffled by the rushing waves.

He'd lost track of time. The tide came in with a force. The current threatened to pull them under.

Caspar caught a quick glimpse of the way Keziah's eyes widened in terror before the waves tore them apart. The next thing he knew, they were both thrust under the water.

The sound of her scream was muffled by their submergence. It was the only thing Caspar could think about as he fought his way back to the surface.

He kicked, ignoring the gruesome feel of hanging skin at the base of his foot as he scanned the rising tides. His breathing was ragged, having been caught off guard by the slip. He treaded water waiting for a glimpse of her.

Where had she gone?

"Keziah?" Caspar called, barely hearing the echo of his own voice above the rushing waves. "Keziah?!" he tried again with more urgency, still treading water as best he could.

"Cas—" he heard finally, catching sight of her only moments before she dipped below the waves.

Caspar's blood ran cold. Without a second thought, he dove beneath the sea, powering towards her as she struggled to break the surface. He reached her quickly, wrapping an arm around her waist and hoisting her back to the shallows. She clung fearfully to his arm and then to his chest, holding on to him as if he were the only thing standing between her and death. Only when they reached the shore did he realise how true the sentiment was.

He felt the heavy beating of her heart against his chest as he scooped her up and carried her safely to shore. She was tense, shaken. Her fingers dug deep into the skin of his arm. As he rested her on the pebbled shore, she took her time in unclawing her fingers from his skin.

The façade of invincibility and fearlessness she'd worn had officially crumbled. The slip had exposed a side of her that he knew she'd never intended for him to see. Caspar remembered the way she'd looked at the water when they'd first arrived, the way she'd frozen as she contemplated it. Even the way she looked at him now, green eyes widened like saucers, filled with deep-rooted fear. Her ragged breath sounded above the roar of the wave. Her eyes rimmed with tears.

He should've known when they'd first arrived. She'd bitten down on her fears for his sake, because she hadn't wanted him to catch on to her secret. He should've realised it then, but he'd been too distracted by his attraction to her to notice the way her mood had shifted, how her spine had straightened in false defiance. She'd remained in the shallows for a reason, but he'd pulled her in deeper. He'd accidentally led her to the edge. And when he'd slipped, her façade cracked. The way she'd flayed about in the water was an instant giveaway.

Keziah couldn't swim.

Caspar knelt beside her on the shore and gazed sympathetically into her eyes. He let the silence fall between them until her breathing settled, giving her the space he knew she required after such a traumatic event. Then, he moved slowly, as if he were working with a wild animal. He opened his arms slowly, allowing her to go at her own pace, to seek comfort in them. He wanted nothing more than to comfort her, to see the fear banished from her eyes.

Suddenly, Keziah embraced him, clasping her arms tightly around his chest. She squeezed, sobbing profusely into his torso.

Caspar wrapped his arms around her gently, allowing her

to find shelter in his embrace. He held onto her through the wave of emotions, until he felt her trembling subside. At that moment, he knew he would do anything for her. He never wished to see her hurt again.

"Why didn't you tell me?" he whispered into the crown of her head when the sobs lessened.

Keziah sniffled. "I... I'm sorry..."

"You have nothing to apologize for," he assured her. "It was my fault. I should've known..." Caspar planted a kiss to her forehead. "I am so sorry, Keziah."

At some point, she pulled away from him, wiping her eyes in her arm. "Your foot..." she said, pointing to the stream of blood washing from his sole to the water.

In truth, he'd forgotten about it. The adrenaline of the experience had taken away the initial pain, but as he stared at the open flap of skin, the stinging sensation returned full force.

"It's nothing," he lied, leaning back onto the sand to take a better look.

"It's not nothing," she chastised, a hint of fear and sadness still lingering in her voice.

He would've repeated himself, but he could tell Keziah needed the distraction, needed to feel in control of something after having the ground pulled out from beneath her.

Caspar sat back patiently, watching as Keziah grabbed one of their discarded articles of clothing and tore off the sleeve. Before he could protest, she grabbed his ankle and began wrapping the fabric around the gash.

Caspar winced at the pain, but he knew she was right to bandage it. He would lose too much blood otherwise. Once they got back, he could look at applying the salve to it. If treated well, it would heal up in a few days. For now, it meant he'd be limping just like his father.

Then, Keziah looked up at him, the fear flushing from her eyes. She bit down on the tentative smile forming at her lips.

"What is it?" he asked, wondering at her sudden change in temperament.

"We're even…" she said before breaking into a laugh.

Caspar looked from his foot to her arm and shook his head.

"I'm glad that amuses you…" he replied, matching her smile hesitantly. He knew she needed something to take her mind off what had transpired, and in this case, he was more than happy to be the butt of the joke. Besides, she had such a charmingly obnoxious laugh, it was hard to be even remotely mad at it.

Accompanying her laugh was the low grumble of the sea, its hunger swelling in the way of a missed meal, a subtle hint that it was time for them to leave. Caspar rose from the ground, shifting his weight tentatively onto his undamaged foot. Keziah followed suit, helping to stabilize him as he dressed.

Caspar watched her working through the evident pain still residing in her arm. The bandage had slid down in the commotion, but the scab over the wound still held. It had drastically improved since he'd first bandaged and applied the poultice to it. He knew the same wonders would be done to his foot.

When she finished dressing herself, Keziah slid an arm beneath his shoulder and nudged him to rest part of his weight on her. For someone so small, she was incredibly sturdy. She helped him the rest of the way out of the cave, allowing the echoes of high tide to fill the silent space between them. All the while, Caspar found himself wondering why she hadn't mentioned to him the fact that she couldn't swim. If he'd known, he would never have put her in such a position. Didn't she know that of him by now?

"I never learned," Keziah whispered out of nowhere.

"What?"

"To swim..." she clarified. Her voice was low; the echoing waves should've swallowed the sound completely. Despite the noise, Caspar's ears had learned to hear only her. And what she'd said startled him. Had she read his mind? When he looked down at her, he found the telltales of embarrassment streaking across her cheeks.

"We don't do things like that where I'm from," she added.

Caspar pursed his lips. Once again, she'd allowed him into her confidences, and once again, he questioned his worthiness. Slowly but surely, the little bits of her he'd been privy to rooted themselves in his heart. She was unwittingly planting a garden there, and he was powerless to stop her.

"You could've told me," was all he managed in reply.

"I'm not so...weak."

Caspar looked at her in awe. At no point in their time together had Caspar ever considered her weak.

"What's weak about not knowing how to swim?"

"It's not that..."

"...are you afraid of the water?"

"It's not that I'm afraid of it..." she grumbled. "Water is beautiful when there's only a bit of it. I love the rain and the way it makes the world smell. I love the small ponds hidden about the forest. I love my baths and the falls... It's just..."

"There's more earth around them," Caspar realized.

Keziah nodded guiltily. "I'm like a stone. I sink."

"I could teach you," Caspar said. When Keziah didn't initially reply, he cleared his throat and added, "to swim."

Keziah looked up at him in disbelief. "Why?" The bite in her tone made him stumble slightly. She helped to steady him before rectifying the harshness of her tone. "I mean, would you?"

"Well, that way…" Why had he offered? If she was only going to leave, to return to her own lands, she wouldn't need to learn at all. Keziah waited for a response. Caspar felt a tightening in his throat. It was just an offer, wasn't it? So, why did she look almost *hopeful*? And why did he feel the same? *Say something, anything. You look ridiculous,* he urged himself. "That way…" He smiled. "You could be the first ever swimming rock," he concluded, hoping a laugh would sway her further.

Keziah blinked up at him. Her silence may have lasted less than a second, but that blank scrutiny had felt eternal. Until, finally, she let out a soft chuckle. He felt her elbow nudge him in the ribs.

"You are a ridiculous man, Caspar."

Caspar felt his heart miss a beat. She said it. For the first time. No hunter, no mocking nickname. *She called me by my name…*

His name spoken in her voice was the sweetest sound he'd ever heard. Somehow, it sounded like a compliment all on its own. It was beautiful. It was yet another reason he couldn't let her go.

After everything that had transpired between them, Caspar had a hard time keeping his thoughts in order, let alone his body. The whole experience remained etched in his memory. His heart scarcely recovering from the shock—the excitement.

But then, as if to dampen the experience, that insufferable voice of reason reminded him he could not let himself get carried away with his feelings.

She isn't here to stay, it said. *No matter what you think you feel, she isn't here to stay.*

He smiled as best he could through it all. Meanwhile, the internal dialogue had his hopes drying up faster than a puddle in the midday sun.

"If it's any consolation…" he began, not wanting to lose what little they had. "I don't think you're weak at all."

Keziah said nothing, but the blush that crept across her cheeks said it all.

As they made their way out of the cave, only the echoes of the retreating wake followed them. Caspar was grateful for the noise, considering the silence and tensions that had settled between them. Their actions had ramifications that neither of them wished to confront. Not now, and if common sense had anything to say about it, not ever.

Still, his heart screamed at him to say something to her, to slay the doubt and insecurities. It fought valiantly against his mind, wishing not to let that moment between them drift into oblivion. In the end, he held his tongue.

Ever since his mother died, Caspar had avoided any kind of affection that he might end up losing. The girls in town had tried to approach him on a fair few occasions. He'd usually thank them for their advances and politely decline any further interaction. It was easier that way. He wouldn't end up disappointing anyone with unreciprocated feelings, and the smaller blow to their egos would usually be patched up by the other lustful men in town. Besides, caring for his father had become a fulltime job, and that spoke nothing of the time taken up by hunting.

But there was something different about Keziah. Something that demanded attention, even in spite of all his precautions against it.

Caspar tried his best to ignore the feelings creeping into his heart. The initial curiosity surrounding her had overnight turned into something more. They had become confidants, sharing secrets they hid from even those closest to them.

Despite their different upbringings and cultures, he felt he could share his thoughts without fear of reproach or judgement. With her brash and brazen nature, she'd demanded his attention, lowered his guard, and, unbeknownst to him in the moment, she'd woven herself into the tapestry of his never-ending thoughts.

The previous night on the roof had only been the beginning of this longing. A taste of intimacy. The precursor to something his heart had been holding out for, and which it reluctantly knew it could never have. But that moment had been special enough to suffice. He would never have been so bold as to ask of life more.

A moment of true understanding. A someone else to share in the suffering that was life. At least he'd gotten that much. A sliver of hope, if nothing else.

That could have been it—that should've been it. The beginnings of a friendship... had their passions not gotten the better of them.

Yet, seeing her, surrounded by the crystalline waters of the hidden oasis, something else bubbled up. Desires of a more carnal nature appeared. No longer could he fight the urge to be next to her, to hold her, to run his fingers through her ebony hair and to trace the outline of her lips with his tongue. Urges that he'd not caught sight of until they were right in front of him.

He avoided looking down at her now, knowing that if he did, he might get trapped in the enchanted forest that was her gaze, and they'd never make it home before dark.

The thump in his heart was loud and restless. He wondered if she might hear it echoing above the roar of the waves. He certainly did. That traitorous heart of his wanted something it knew very well it could never have. He hadn't noticed the tension building in his body, or the nervous frown slowly taking root on his cheeks until Keziah nudged him again.

"Are you alright?" she asked, clearing her throat to ensure a clearer sound. Her voice had regained its usual tactless bluntness, but the concern that resided in it was genuine. "You're stiffer than an oak trunk."

"A what?"

"You know… The trees with the nuts that you grind to make flour?"

"You mean the Carob trees?" he corrected, garnering him one of those spinetingling, all-encompassing laughs of hers. Caspar furrowed his brow at her. "What?"

As her laugh settled, she nudged him a final time. This time, it was a gentle jab. A subtle acknowledgement that the whole situation had become too serious between them, and that she still wished to remain light-hearted.

"There you go again with your made-up words…"

"I…" He wanted to correct her. He wanted to let her know that she didn't know as much as she thought she did. But, when he looked down into her bright green eyes, he realised she already knew this. It wasn't a comment against him; she'd done it *for* him.

His response remained on the tip of his tongue as the rest of him fell deeper into the trap of her gaze. Despite the adequacy of his education—at least compared to the other boys in his village—Caspar found there was a quality to her that he couldn't quite describe but wished he could. It wasn't just the way her eyes glimmered with the freshness of a thousand desert limes, or that her hair shone the glossy black of the cold night sky, or even that her skin was as soft as fresh clay. No. These were merely the superficial things that he knew time would take, as it had of his mother many years prior. Features that, in all honesty, had never been idolized by the people of his village. But, if he looked past what the eyes could see and gave in to what only his heart could envision, Keziah became so much more than a meagre sum of features. More than a sum of poetic but insignificant descriptors.

First and foremost, there was her laugh, a roar no desert cat could compete with nor sunlight outshine. A laugh as obnoxious as the howling wind through the canyons, yet as loving as nightfall, as friendly as a crackling bonfire beneath a sky full of stars, and as timeless as the stories shared around it.

Then, her ferocity, matched only by the unrelenting desert heat, but which, when paired with her kind heart, could just as easily make flowers grow in scorched earth. What fuelled her, he knew not, but he was sure that with it, she could do anything she set her mind to. That, topped off with her stubbornness that could make a mountain move— and probably had—would ensure success in all endeavours. It was a quality that demanded respect, a respect he would gladly give, for he'd more than seen its merit.

Still, not even these could aptly sum up the beauty of

Keziah. All the little things that she'd revealed to him, slowly, had turned his ever-cautious heart to mush around her. Like the unfurling petals of the cactus flowers that later give way to their sweet berries, Keziah's inner spark came as a surprise, a gift, a blessing he might have missed out on had he let his prejudice win over his heart.

In that moment, Caspar spoke two silent prayers to fate. The first, a prayer of gratitude for having allowed them to cross paths. The second, a wish that their star-crossed union not be in vain. Because, if he allowed himself to be honest, to want with the fervent passion and ignorance of a child, he would no longer fight the feelings he harboured for her.

* * *

They hobbled home as best they could, the injured pair of them. The conversations that accompanied them throughout the walk could have been interpreted as trivial to an outsider, but Caspar hung on to her every word.

Keziah remarked on the strange, transient quality of the soil beneath her feet. Caspar knew that, coming from anyone else, he'd not hear a word of something so inconsequential to him, but from her, he'd hear hours upon hours of facts about dirt. He knew how important it was to her because of the nature of her powers, which meant that a part of him wanted it to be important for him too. And the more he heard about it, the more he realised that maybe it *should* be more important to him.

Where she came from, the ground held on to moisture. It was dense and soft, or so she said, and it wouldn't cause such a strain on the spine while one walked. She called it a foot hug, which made him laugh. In contrast, she claimed the dust in his lands was harsh. The top layer shifted with the winds. It was unfriendly. At best, it slipped beneath one's feet. At worst, she surprisingly predicted it could drift upwards and, if the wind was strong enough, fly into one's eyes and nose. He figured it best not to tell her how apt her prediction had been. She'd been scared enough by the beach already to alert her to the terrible threat of dust storms.

Their conversation about dirt lasted the entirety of their walk—which worked out in his favour. Otherwise, he would have to contend with the nagging delusions in his head about the future he could have with Keziah, and he didn't want to entertain such thoughts. It would be like adding logs to a burning fire, but this particular fire already had enough fuel to last a lifetime after their steamy encounter. Even thinking about it now sent blood flowing to places it shouldn't and hope to a heart that shouldn't want it… but admittedly did.

They managed to make it back to the house before the sun grazed the tops of the canyons. At this time of year, the days were already growing short. At the peak of summer, one could make the trek north through the desert and hit the nearest town by midnight on foot. Nowadays, nightfall would come before one had made it past the halfway oasis, leading to a journey that would take well into the dawn.

To add insult to injury, his father waited for them at the door with a more pronounced scowl on his face. Those predatory eyes of his glinted with disappointment at the sight of him draped over Keziah's shoulders and dropped immediately to the bandage on his foot.

Keziah slowed her stride, having noticed the disgust directed at her. Caspar didn't want her to fear anything ever again, especially not after what had happened to her. His romantic feelings for her aside, she had become a friend, and he would never let a friend suffer.

❦ CHAPTER 10 ❦

TO SAY THE DAY HAD NOT TURNED OUT THE way Keziah had planned was an understatement at best. She'd lost herself to both pride and then passion. She'd almost drowned. She'd broken down in ways she'd never done in front of anyone before. She'd forsaken the last semblance of pride within her.

And yet, she couldn't help herself from smiling.

Through it all, Caspar had stayed by her side. He'd held her throughout the barrage of waves. He'd seen her in her weakest moment… and he didn't think less of her.

If she had been home, someone would have commented on her childish shows of emotion. She wasn't supposed to fear, and certainly not another element. The people of her nation were supposed to have a will as strong as iron, nerves as sharp as steel, skin as hard as diamonds. They were not supposed to be as flaky and foolish as some of the other peoples of Visanthe. And they were certainly not supposed to cry in the arms of anyone.

Or so they claimed. But Caspar had shattered all the notions of strength to which she'd clung. For the first time in her life, Keziah was forced to question the soundness of her people's reasoning.

Conversation between them was sparse as they made their way back through the tunnel. The intimacy of their moment had left her at a loss for words. She felt responsible for his limp and the gash on his foot, but he didn't appear to hold it against her—which made it all the worse. At this point, the offenses against her were racking up. She'd created a rift between him and his father, she'd all but destroyed their washing station, she'd hurt him. Caspar had so many reasons to hate her. But his actions couldn't be further from hate.

He checked in on her. He made sure she felt safe, comfortable. He tended to her wounds. And now, he wanted to teach her to swim. She'd feared the distress in her eyes after the incident might have disgusted him, but it had the opposite effect. Keziah doubted she'd be able to unfeel the warmth of his hands on her back, the beat of his heart against her ear, the softness of his lips against hers.

She doubted she would be able to unfeel him ever again.

Even now, their proximity had her heart in a state. It fluttered like a hummingbird, trapped in her chest. The silence between them only amplified its noise. She hated how the trauma had bonded her to him.

Having Caspar draped over her shoulders in this way was a blessing and a curse. Keziah's traitorous heart wanted nothing more than to be close to him, but she knew that, at some point, this fantasy would dry up. Just like the desert around them.

Tucked under his arm, the occasional waft of Caspar's

scent drifted into her nose—burnt wood and lavender, with just a touch of sea salt from their escapade. The familiarity of the lavender brought her comfort; it reminded her of home. The burnt wood, however, was so different, so complimentary, so uniquely him. Keziah hated to admit it, but she found his scent so inviting, she wished to bury her nose in the fabric of his clothes. The thought alone had her avoiding his gaze out of sheer embarrassment.

By the time they emerged from the cave, the afternoon sun had fallen over the lands. The silence had worn her down to the point where she needed to fill it with something—anything. Sadly, that anything ended up being nothing less than dirt.

The nerves had gotten to her so completely that the only thing she could confidently speak about was dirt. Keziah gave Caspar an in-depth lecture on the differences between that of his lands versus that of her own. To his credit, Caspar listened attentively, asking questions that not even she had thought to ask because... not even she found the subject as interesting as he seemed to.

With his occasional laughs, Caspar seemed to be enjoying their time together as much as she was. As they walked, the separations between them fell flat. They were not *Argia* and *Harri*, not *kanala* and hunter; they were simply boy and girl, Caspar and Keziah, two people relishing in each other's company—teetering on the edge of attraction.

This thought alone had Keziah's insides in knots. Something had begun to grow between them. It grew slowly, the way the saplings claw through layers of dirt, not quite visible upon first glances—or seconds... or thirds. But it was there.

Perhaps it had been all along. A little seed that needed

nourishment. Soils that had long since dried out were being tended to with each interaction. Needless to say, after their escapade, everything had changed. Their proximity had nourished it—whatever it was—and the greedy little thing only continued to demand more. The roots of it, feeble as they may have been, anchored this sapling to their hearts.

Iturri help me, Keziah thought to herself.

The sun shone down on them as though it too wanted to feed the growing fires of desire. As though it wished to show its approval of the pairing.

When they arrived at the door, the illusion of happiness shattered.

Beneath the aged wooden pagoda at the entrance to the hut, Caspar's father waited for them with a frown set as deep as the grooves of the canyons around them. The light of the afternoon sun marked the lines on his face with shadow and highlighted the irritation in his eyes. His predatory gaze bounced from her to Caspar, and then down to Caspar's foot, which was still bandaged and bloodied.

Keziah unconsciously hung back as she met his eyes. The scrutiny and blame in his expression were knives to her chest. Caspar squeezed at her arm in reassurance, but she remained cautious. Every encounter with him had left her at the receiving end of attacking insults. There were only so many blows to her ego she could take before lashing out in retaliation, but she tried her best to remain calm. This man was frail but not fearful, and he certainly would not go down without a fight. He looked as if he were about to comment on the state of their arrival when Caspar beat him to it.

"Father, it was an accident," he said, his voice swelling as if preparing for a shouting match.

"I am tired of trying to convince you of her danger," his

father scoffed in reply. "If you are content to live with the pain she brings, you are free to do so…" he added before hobbling back into his rooms.

Keziah felt Caspar release the wind from his chest. The battle was over before it had even begun, and yet, the damage was done regardless.

If the insults had left bruises, his indifference left gashes. With it, Keziah felt as though she were not human enough to be addressed, that she was no better than the invisible antagonists of the stories that parents told their children before bed. A cautionary tale that held no true weight over reality. A thing to be forgotten within the next fortnight.

Keziah furrowed her brow, wondering why now, why those words had left her more damaged and degraded than when Caspar had scored her with his arrow.

"Don't listen to him," Caspar said as he prodded her to keep moving. The light smile on his face meant he'd thought he'd gotten through to his father. But Keziah knew better than to consider him won over.

In truth, the indifference hurt most because it was the most foreign thing she'd encountered. In her own lands, people shouted and carried on until a matter was resolved. It may have seemed counterintuitive, but the shouting and verbalizing of pain was an act of love—or at least, that's how she'd grown up registering it.

This indifference was different. Terrible. It meant she was not even worth putting up a fight over. It was not just an absence of love; it was the absence of will—it was the removal of her own voice by the retraction of another's. And if that weren't enough, the words themselves made the rounds in her mind, to the point where she truly began to wonder if Caspar's father was right.

She'd clogged their bathing stream; she'd sliced his foot—albeit indirectly. She'd driven a wedge between Caspar and his father and was a strain on their already limited resources.

Was it true? Did she only bring suffering? Caspar's kindness was abundant, but even she knew her presence would only continue to cause him pain.

As if reading the concern on her face, Caspar rested a hand on her shoulder. Concern knotted his brow as he looked down at her.

"Hey," he began, his voice riddled with that strangely comforting Caspar-kindness she was beginning to grow accustomed to. "Breathe."

Keziah cocked an eyebrow. "What?"

"Take a deep breath," he insisted.

"Why?"

"You are trying to fight too many battles at once. I can see it in your eyes. You've got your sights set on too many targets." His hand raised to gently caress her hair. The feel of his fingers grazing over her scalp quelled her racing mind. "So, breathe. Pick a single target. Nock your arrow. Release that breath and let it go. You'll only wear yourself down otherwise."

Keziah could do little more than hold his gaze, and even that was becoming a challenge. Nothing he'd said before had ever made such an impact on her as this. He'd seen them, the fights within. A boy with whom she'd spent less than a fortnight had seen what not even her family had in all her sixteen years. His kind words threatened her with a storm of tears, but she'd already done more than enough crying for the day.

She did as she was told, taking the air fully into her lungs and releasing slowly.

Caspar smiled. "Better?"

She nodded. "How did you learn to do that?"

"Trick of the trade. As a hunter, you learn to choose a single target and give it all your focus. If you keep your mind on more than one prey at a time, you lose them all."

Caspar took her hands in his and twirled her around so that she leaned against his chest. He raised her arms, mimicking the act of nocking an arrow into a bow, his body hovering around hers in a tentative embrace. They aimed at the backyard, at the unfinished garden, then at the kitchen, and the bedroom, before finally settling on a bird that had landed on the pagoda. Then, Caspar leaned in closer, whispering the next part in her ear as they drew back their imaginary bowstring.

"Once you do, you take a breath to slow your heart."

Keziah did as she was told, breathing fully into her lungs again as best she could. Caspar seemed content with her imitation of breath. What he didn't realise was that having him there, so close, so intimately close, made her heart want to break free of her chest and race towards the sun. She closed her eyes, focusing on the feel of the air in her lungs, and the sound of his soft voice beside her ear.

"Take your time," he added. "There's no rush. Breathe until it all fades."

Slowly but surely, she started to feel her heart steady. The familiar hum of focus rippled across her skin. This technique Caspar taught her was not unlike her own tapping into the feel of the ground. Each time she'd tried to move the stones around her, this was the feeling she sought. Sometimes she would get it, other times… Well, she rightly sounded like the large creature Caspar had hoped to find at the sharp end of his arrow when they'd first met. She'd thought this feeling elusive, but here, with no powers, Caspar could access it so easily.

"Now, breathe out and…" he added, opening the hand with the imaginary bowstring.

Guided by his gentle voice, Keziah opened her eyes and mimicked his actions. When she released her imaginary arrow, she noticed the world no longer seemed so loud. Her thoughts had quelled. She had reached that very state of calm that had eluded her for so long.

"How?" she asked simply, for those were all the words she could manage.

"Not everything is force. A fire confined has many uses. With only one log to feed it, it gives warmth, allows us to cook, brightens a room, and when it has served its purpose, it will go out on its own. On the contrary, if we scatter logs about the place, we risk burning down all that we have. A fire with no containment, no control, brings only destruction." He tapped a finger to her forehead and added, "And thoughts, if left untended, can spiral and consume you just the same."

"I never thought about it that way…" she admitted as a blush crept into her cheeks.

Caspar shrugged. "I guess you don't until you have to…"

There it is again, she thought. A hint of vulnerability. Keziah had a feeling it had something to do with his childhood, and potentially, his mother. She would've liked to ask after it, but she held her tongue. If he had been anyone else, she might not have spared it a second thought; the words would've flown from her lips faster than she could process them.

But with Caspar, things were different. She was different.

Noticing the shift in his mood and not wanting to end the day on such notes, Keziah brandished her best smile and turned to the kitchen.

"Speaking of fires and food…" she began.

Caspar laughed. "Alright, I get it."

They took turns in quickly washing up before the skies grew dark and the night cold before settling back into the kitchen.

Caspar strode over to the counter and began gathering the dried meat trimmings from the previous night, along with all sorts of roots and tubers.

Keziah shuffled in alongside him, silently watching closely as Caspar carried out this most basic of household tasks. She leaned over the counter, resting her chin in her palm as she contemplated him. The speed with which he moved the knife over the produce spoke of experience. The rhythmic click of the metal over the wooden cutting board spoke of passion. Yet another trait of his which piqued her interest.

"Do you like to cook?" she asked, twirling the length of her braid around with her free hand.

"I do," he replied, tossing the produce into a pan.

"I can tell."

"Oh?"

"It wouldn't taste good if you didn't."

Beneath the shadows of his gentle auburn curls, Keziah spied a smirk on his lips.

"You think my cooking tastes good?" he asked, turning from the cutting board to the pot again and stirring.

Keziah fought the smile that wanted to spread across her

face. Between hunger and the strange soup of emotions swirling around within her, she felt a curious sense of camaraderie with the vegetables. Hearing the coy sound of satisfaction in his voice sent her back into her usual taunting. "Well, it's not terrible…"

Caspar strode over to her with a spoon, cupping his hand beneath to avoid spillage. "Taste this."

With a slightly cocked brow, Keziah obeyed. The flavours swirling around on her palate from the albeit usually plain vegetables brought a sigh to her lips, one that seemed to please Caspar more than any words ever would.

"Not terrible, eh?"

Keziah wiped a bit of sauce from her lips, finding it harder to fight the smile. "It's passable," she replied, unable to hide the traces of delight in her tone. In truth, he'd done it again. The resulting stew was better than anything she'd had in her own village, even with the quality of prime material they were working with. Caspar's seasonings and careful hands had turned peasant food into something she would dream about for the rest of her life.

"High praise coming from you," Caspar said with a smile.

Keziah raised her chin at him. "Don't get used to it."

Caspar let out a soft laugh. "I'll try not to." He turned back to the pot on the stove, and Keziah found herself allowing the smile to settle across her face, along with a warm blush.

They spent the rest of the night in quiet contemplation of each other, moving from the kitchen to the roof. The intention was to stare up at the stars like the previous night, only nothing was like the previous night.

Neither of them wished to admit it, but they maintained

a bashful distance from each other. The heated intimacy of their time at the beach lingered around them, though neither made moves to acknowledge it. Part of Keziah feared she'd lost the chance at further intimacy the moment he'd seen her cry. The other part simply reminded her she wasn't meant to be there in the first place. Their meeting was a fluke, an accident, a mistake of fate. And since Caspar had not acknowledged what had transpired between them, she felt obliged to do the same, though her heart yearned for the contrary.

"If you could go anywhere in the world, regardless of nation, where would you go?" Keziah asked, wishing to fill the heavy silence with something other than tension. She sat perched on the edge of the roof like the night before. She stretched her toes, the desert night's winds tickling the soles of her feet as she stared up at the stars. Goosebumps raced down her arms, though she could just as well attribute them to his proximity as she could the cold.

"I've never given it much thought…" Caspar replied as he dangled his legs over the lip of the roof beside hers. "I've never really imagined myself away from the village."

"Never?" She turned to him in shock, her brow furrowed. Keziah had so often contemplated escaping the forest that she found it hard to believe someone could be so content with their own home—especially one so admittedly lacking as Caspar's.

"What about the cities of Osiir? Or the isles of snow and ice? Or the pillar mountains in the lands of the wind?"

There were so many places that Keziah had heard about in tales from the elders of her tribe that had captured her heart. Embarrassingly, even the burning red soils of the desert had fascinated her as a child. But she had never been allowed to leave the confines of the forest. The furthest she'd ever gotten was the river crossing into the next tribe's territory. Keziah could not fathom how Caspar, who had all the freedom in the world to get up and go to wherever his heart desired, was content to stay.

"I can't imagine leaving any of this behind..." he whispered, staring not at the stars but down at the half-finished garden.

Keziah was about to comment on how he could find gardens a hundred times better than his in the other lands, but when she looked at him, she noticed something that gave her pause. A crease had formed at his brow. His legs too had stopped swinging. His tone had become almost melancholic. She looked out over the garden as well, wondering what had changed his tune so completely from before, when she remembered what he'd first told her.

The garden belonged to his mother.

A deep-rooted ache clawed its way up in her chest. The garden was a placeholder for the woman he could never see again, never touch again. For the woman whose love he would never feel again.

The shadows of the past clung readily to him. He walked around as though he was immune to it, but the pain was there, unyielding. Keziah remembered the way he'd clung to the knife at the market stall. That must have belonged to her too. All around the house were trinkets left back from a different time, one unmarred by shadows.

Keziah had lost her mother before she could walk, let alone crawl. Memories of her were few and far between. But Caspar? The memories of his mother were everywhere. Her ghost lingered in the very walls of the house.

Out of instinct, Keziah nestled herself closer to him.

After all they'd been through, she figured this was the least offensive thing she'd done to him thus far. She rested her head on his shoulder, unsure of what to say to comfort him, but wanting him to know she was present.

She smiled at the weight of his head leaning against hers.

"But then…" he whispered. "The world is vast, isn't it? Perhaps that is the point…"

"I'm not sure I know what you mean."

"We must do things of which we know little, lest we stay trapped in comfort's cage."

"There you go again on your poetic tangents," she said to lighten the mood, hoping to keep the sadness from his heart. "It would do you good to get out, less wallowing, more adventuring."

Caspar chuckled. "Oh? And what would you suggest?"

"Something thrilling," Keziah replied, lifting herself off his shoulder. She scanned his gaze for signs of raised spirits. Though his eyes reflected the gentle blue hue of starlight, she found no melancholy in them, only curiosity.

"Hunting is thrilling…" he said with a smirk.

Keziah rolled her eyes. "Something you've never done before."

Caspar ran his fingers through his hair, pondering the idea with a soft "hmm" when she noticed his eyes begin to glow with mischief. "You're right…" he replied, decided in his words. So much so that she questioned her own.

"About what exactly?"

Caspar stretched his neck and rose from his perch, extending his arm out to help her stand. Keziah looked at it questioningly.

"Will you trust me?" he asked.

This time, she didn't hesitate.

❧ CHAPTER 11 ❧

THE TOWN BY DAY WAS A BUSTLING pandemonium of sight, smell, and sound; by night, these broad strokes of chaos became a masterpiece. Torches hung from each wall, burning a welcoming orange that spilled from the chipped white walls to the dusty streets, creating the effect of red rivers running through the town. The maze of covered stalls in the marketplace had been removed, leaving only simple food stalls on the outskirts. The centre of the marketplace was occupied by a wooden stage, atop which sat a young woman in a meditative pose. She was clad in a deep blood red—the only coloured fabric for miles.

The crowds gathered around her.

Caspar used his gait to carve a path to the front of the stage, one hand on her back to guide her, the other nudging the rest of the patrons out of their way.

Keziah had initially hesitated when Caspar suggested a return to the town, after seeing the way the boys had reacted to her initially, but Caspar assured her he would not let anyone harm her. This time, she was fully cloaked, both to fend of the chill of the desert night, and to mask her foreign features. Still, the fear in her simmered.

Around them, the crowd grew impatient.

"What are we waiting for?" Keziah asked, agitation lacing her voice. She'd tried to swallow it down, but it wouldn't stay put. Each unexpected sound, each shove from another patron had her more rigid than a fence post. The ground trembled from all the shifting feet around them. Her shoulder muscles pulled taught. They irritated the wound on her arm, but the adrenaline coursing through her was enough distraction from the pain.

Suddenly, she felt Caspar's warm, gentle hand settle over her shoulder. He squeezed reassuringly. At no point did he attempt to remove it. Instead, he drew himself in closer behind her. Such a small gesture compared to their escapade at the beach, and yet, it had her heart in a flutter. She was happy to have the billowing fabric cloaking her, for it hid the blush burning across her cheeks.

Caspar leaned over and whispered in her ear, "Something neither of us have ever experienced before."

As if by the command of his words, sultry music began to play. A rhythmic drum, light metal chiming, something that sounded like rainfall, and a stringed instrument made up the choir. The crowd settled, halting the low tremor in the ground. A final instrument, a mystical-sounding flute, joined in. At the sound of it, the girl opened her eyes.

She flickered to life, stretching her arms up high and twirling them above her head, mimicking flames. Then, she leapt from her perch, and as the music got louder, faster, her dance followed suit. Bells on her ankles and wrists gave voice to each of her movements. Each swish, a cascade of metal. She danced without a care in the world. The drums commanded her hips, the flute her arms, and her eyes… Keziah realized they were entirely lost to the ecstasy of the music.

The song ended as the woman dropped to her knees, her wide red skirt flayed out beneath her like a pool of blood. The modest clapping from the audience was at odds with what Keziah thought the performance deserved, but she wasn't about to start the hollering herself.

"Should we go?" she whispered, resting a hand over the one Caspar had left on her shoulder.

"Just wait," he replied, pulling her in closer to him.

Her body had relaxed significantly since the beginning of the dance. She allowed him to guide it backwards to lean against his chest. All the while, she waited, noticing that none of the other patrons had left. Instead, a larger crowd had gathered beyond.

Then, two men appeared at either side of the woman carrying torches, one burning a bright orange, the other a vibrant green. They slotted them into holes in the stage and promptly made their exit before the music started up again. This time, the crowd began hollering even before the woman raised her head.

The next dance was unlike anything Keziah had ever witnessed in her lifetime. The music came in harder. The flames shot up into the night sky. The woman rose surrounded by sparks. Her blonde hair came loose, rippling in the breeze. Sweat pooled on her brow, glistening like gemstones above her eyes.

And then, she began to twirl.

The flames followed her movements, extending out in bursts and waves, always coming back to a ball between her palms. She bent the colours, meshed them together and ripped them apart in time with the music. When Keziah next caught a glimpse of her eyes, she found a woman unbound by a soul.

She all element, all fire, caged in skin and bone.

She was *kanala.*

Keziah's eyes widened. This was the first time she'd ever seen an *Argia kanala* before. From that point on, she heard nothing but the music and the slow crackling of the flames.

The woman's powers were transfixing. This element, the one she'd long feared for its ferocity, danced like any woman of flesh and blood, weaving its way through the air around the woman. It rose and fell with the music, warming the cold desert night. At some point, the woman had even fashioned it into the shape of a giant serpent.

Keziah hadn't realized her jaw had dropped until Caspar squeezed her shoulder once more. She turned to look up at him, eager to tear his gaze from the spectacle and share her excitement, but found his eyes already fixed on her.

"Are you enjoying it?" he said, his voice barely audible over the box drum and chimes.

Keziah nodded and quickly returned her gaze to the performance. *How long has he been staring at me?* she wondered, biting down on the smile at her lips.

For the rest of the performance, she found only part of her attention was on the woman and the flames. The other part resided in the little part of her shoulder that Caspar now ran his thumb over. Unlike the protective hold he'd had on her before, this one made her stomach twist. When the performance ended and the crowds began to disperse, Keziah found herself wishing for a lot more than a simple graze of his thumb.

"How did you like it?" he asked as they made their way back down the paths towards his house.

"It was incredible," she mumbled, trying to contain the full extent of her joy. "I didn't know fire could be so beautiful…"

Caspar chuckled, letting his hand fall to the lower part of her back as they walked. "Fire is but a tool, and a tool bears only the will of its master."

"I suppose you're right…" she replied half-heartedly. Her mind remained on the patch of her back covered by billowing cotton and the light pressure of his hand. A small part of her heart burned, though she knew it came from no illness. The little ember she'd held in her heart for him flickered to life, but by now, it was no longer an ember. It was a full-blown flame, comparable to any the woman wielded in the night's performance.

The rest of the walk was spent in silence, though Keziah's mind held none of it. By the time they returned, her mental chatter had become too much to leave unvoiced.

"Had you already seen the performance before?" she asked.

"My parents used to take me," he replied.

"But you said we were doing something neither of us had done before. You've already seen the show. So…?"

Caspar smiled, though she swore she could see a blush creeping into his cheeks as well. "Well, you'd never seen fire dance, and I'd never had anyone I'd wanted to show it to. I think that counts for thrilling new experiences on both sides, wouldn't you?"

Keziah was too stunned to speak. She nodded, following him to the door of the bedroom. She pressed her back to the door as he hovered over her. Their eyes locked. The air vanished from her lungs. She waited…

"I'm glad you had a good time," he said, his voice hoarse.

"Likewise," was all she could manage.

"We should probably get to bed," he added.

"I agree," she replied.

Yet, neither of them made to separate.

They stared into each other's eyes for what felt like an eternity. The fire in his gaze had returned. Her heartbeat echoed in her ears. She caught his lip quivering slightly. He leaned in a touch, she mirrored him. Keziah could see he was just as confused at their unspoken treaty as she was. They still hadn't spoken of the beach, but she knew the memory of their passion lingered in his heart as much as hers. Yet, through all the magnetism, they held back. Watching. Waiting for signs from the other on what to do next.

Slowly, he raised his hand to the side of her face, sweeping away a lock of her hair that had freed itself from her covering. He tucked it behind her ear with care, mouth agape as if to speak, but no words came. His hand lingered there for only a moment longer before he dropped it, brows furrowed.

"It has been an…eventful…day," he said, swallowing hard on the ball in his throat.

"It has," she replied, equally as tense.

"I suppose you must be tired…"

"I suppose…"

He took a deep inhale and sighed.

"Goodnight," he said finally.

Her heart sank. "You too…"

It took another long moment for someone to finally move, but in the end, he pulled away first.

"Sleep well," he said, already turning from her.

"And you," she whispered, watching him stalk towards the sofa with defeat resting on his shoulders. She closed the door softly behind him, letting out a heavy sigh.

He wasn't the only one, she thought to herself. *He felt it too.*

She fluffed her pillow and tossed herself onto the straw mattress in frustration. She tossed and turned, her mind returning to each of his touches—gentle or otherwise. Her heart ached with longing in a way she'd never experienced before. All this time, he'd been the answer to her prayers, her liberation. And she knew he felt the same. The distance between them, though small, was torture. Beyond the door lay the object of her deepest desire—not just her passion.

Had it just been passion, I wouldn't be alone tonight…

❧ CHAPTER 12 ❧

THE BED WAS JUST AS UNCOMFORTABLE AS ever, but its floor-like consistency was not the thing that had kept Keziah tossing and turning for most of the night. Her eyes bounced from the wall on one side to the door on the opposite side of the room. The back and forth of her mind keeping time with her swaying.

She wanted to be outside with him.

She didn't want to get attached.

She wanted to thank him again for saving her life.

She knew she should keep conversations to a minimum.

But they were becoming friends.

But it would never work.

But what if it did?

But, but, but…

All the tossing and turning got her nowhere. She found no good way to reconcile the two sides in her mind. At most, it would leave her with a headache in the morning.

"Ugh, why me…" she grumbled into the darkness.

As if in response, she noticed a small beam of white light filtering in through the window. Keziah hustled to her feet to locate its source.

The giant closing eye in the sky had appeared. The moon. The beacon for creatures that prowled the forest. She wondered what was happening in her village, if they had sent huntsmen out to find her, or if they thought she'd been eaten by wolves. She would have to get back soon; her father would not rest until he found her—or at least her corpse.

Keziah rested her elbows on the sill and stared off into the distance. How far was she from home? From here, she couldn't even see the edge of the canyons, and she remembered there was a whole desert beyond the rock walls. She wouldn't even know which direction to head out in. She stared up at the moon again, glowering at the way it seemed to smile at her.

"You're a very strange god. I can't believe Caspar's people pray to you…" Keziah paused, as if waiting for some sort of retribution. When none came, she sighed. "I thought so. You hold no power over me…"

She slumped back down, resting her chin against her fist as she gazed out the window. Her eyes danced over the unfinished garden. They'd made decent work of it in the little time they'd spent, but there was still more to do. Caspar's mood had shifted so drastically before, and she knew it wasn't just over an unfinished garden.

Keziah couldn't bring his mother back, but she wished to at least give him back the garden he'd allowed her death to take. Not to mention the bathing stream she'd accidentally blocked.

All in all, she figured that if she couldn't sleep, she might make good use of her nervous energy.

Keziah crept towards the door, resting her hands upon it gently. It creaked open with little more than a touch. She cringed at the sound, hoping not to wake the rest of the house with her late-night activities. She waited a breath or two, listening out for the sounds of stirring. When none came, Keziah continued out towards the garden.

She passed Caspar, fast asleep on the couch, a handwoven blanket draped over his lanky form. He looked as though he too had tossed and turned most of the night before eventually falling asleep in the most uncomfortable of positions.

Keziah smiled. Even while sleeping he was awkward. She cast a quick glance over at the closed door on the opposite end of the salon. His father had barely spoken to her since their arrival, and any words that had crossed his harsh lips had been colder than the desert night. He had not stirred during their time in the kitchen, and now, well past waking hours, she doubted he would cause a problem for her.

Still, she froze, holding out for his hatred. The irrational fear of the hobbling old man's words had gotten to her.

When she was certain no one had woken, Keziah slipped out into the night and wandered out into the back garden. The cool desert air sent shivers down her arms and spine. It howled as it weaved through the canyons and around the house. She wished she'd brought out a shawl to cover herself, but the work would hopefully warm her up soon enough.

The moon cast shadows across the floor from the various rocks and tools scattered about the yard. Otherwise, the world was quiet, still.

The vegetable patch they'd worked on all morning waited for a final tilling and a scattering of seeds to be completed. They had made so much progress that morning, it was impossible not to smile at how it was turning out. Yet, a heavy sigh escaped her lips as she contemplated it, remembering how her helping had already ruined one thing for Caspar and his father. Keziah worried that if she tried to finish the job, she might end up destroying their progress, like she had with the fountain.

Breathe… Pick a target… said a little whisper in her head which had borrowed Caspar's voice.

The water in the stream had grown stagnant. Beside it were some discarded tools from what she assumed was Caspar's father's attempt at reopening the channel she'd closed. The tools were primitive things, but they seemed to have removed enough of the debris from the inner channel to get a small trickle of water down the rock face.

The winds picked up around her, sending shivers down her arms. The whistle of it came as a blessing, a way to hide the noise of her efforts. Keziah cast a quick glance upwards. The moon, she thought, seemed to be smiling down on her.

Perhaps you have some power after all…

Keziah glanced back at the house quickly to make sure no one had followed her out. When she turned back to the stream again, she was determined to do right by Caspar's father, to fix her mistake, to prove that she was not the nuisance he'd made her out to be.

She took a quick peek at the wound beneath her bandages. Her arm was healing nicely, and the salt water seemed to have done wonders for the wound. She flexed her fingers, feeling only a slight strain up her arm. She knew she would make easy work of it this time.

This time, I will not fail, she thought to herself before moving to strike.

She raised her fist to the rock face and punched the air in front of it. The rock groaned in response, but she was yet to see the results. She tried again, this time noticing a few wayward pebbles fall at her sides.

As expected, the wind muffled the sound of each hit. Keziah would not be deterred. She worked tirelessly, finding part of her soul renewed with each chink she took out of the rock. The same powers she'd been barred from using in her own lands now filled her lungs, her heart.

Her spirit.

Then, to her surprise, the crack in the wall widened. She could sense the debris shifting from within the channel as well.

Almost… But she wasn't ready to get her hopes up. Not yet. She needed to ensure that the channel was clear enough that the waterways would never get blocked again.

Keziah took a deep breath, closing her eyes and focusing on the stone. She could still feel the water rushing from behind the rockface. Its vibrations reverberated through the stone and crept towards her feet. She angled herself in a way that would keep her grounded throughout the process—the way Caspar had taught her.

A single target, she told herself, before thrusting her fist towards the rock—again, and again, and again…

Finally, from behind the stone, she heard a loud crack over the wind, and then another in succession. She took a step back. Before she knew it, the stream began to flow once more with renewed force.

She'd done it—she'd really done it.

Keziah jumped up and down, celebrating her triumph.

She could hardly believe it. If only Caspar could see her now… He had been right. She wasn't weak at all.

"You're up late," a voice growled from behind.

Keziah's breath hitched in her lungs. She turned to find Caspar's father contemplating the stream's new flow. The scowl on his face cut her celebration short. Keziah righted herself, bobbing her head in acknowledgement of his presence. The mere sight of him set her nerves on edge. She knew there was nothing he could do to harm her, and yet, his presence had her spine straighter than a beam.

"You don't belong here…" he said, sparing no love as he addressed her.

"So you've mentioned," Keziah replied stoically. She kept her head high, but his words cut deep. She couldn't tell whether this was the beginning of a new fight or the end of an old one. She bit down on the emotions bubbling up in her chest. She wouldn't let him see her hurt—she couldn't.

"Yet, without you, we might have starved," he concluded before she could get another word in.

Keziah furrowed her brow, unable to hide the shock in her eyes. His acknowledgement was akin to having a pail of cold water poured unceremoniously over her.

Caspar's father refused to meet her gaze, instead maintaining his contemplation of the fountain. There was, however, a subtle difference in the way he gazed upon it now. Keziah spied it almost instantly, the reluctant appreciation.

She didn't expect a "thank you." They were still worlds away from pleasantries. But this was at least a step in the right direction.

"I do not like you," he added softly, letting the words settle between them. He cast a glance over at the house where Caspar slept soundly. A pained sigh escaped his lips. "But you make him smile. He has not smiled this way in a long time." This time, he turned back to her, addressing her in a way he had not since her arrival: as a person. "The women of your tribe are beguiling, meddlesome…"

"It is one thing for you to insult me behind closed doors, but I will not sit and endure insult to my face—" she began, hints of injured pride creeping into her trembling voice.

"Strong-willed, stubborn…" he rattled on undeterred.

"I am not—" She felt the heat rushing to her cheeks.

"And, like her, you put up a good fight."

"I—" Keziah froze, the burning fluster doused by the sudden realization. Her heart stilled.

A heavy silence fell between them. Even the blustering winds died down, as if they too wished to be privy to the conversation.

Caspar's father pursed his lips. His hand clutched tight to the old wooden cane. He trembled, though he tried his best to hide it.

"She had no powers to speak of—other than a sharp tongue and sharper wit," he added. The tightness in his voice hinted at sorrow, but he pushed through it without shedding a tear. "It is…hard…to have someone like her in the house again."

So, Caspar's mother was… Harri?

Keziah furrowed her brow, realizing now how devastating her arrival must have been for him. But then, the story went both ways, didn't it? How come she'd never heard of a woman from her tribe leaving to be with an *Argia*? Surely, someone would've mentioned it. Some obscure reference, an anecdote, something. Right?

She let the anger flow from her in a single heavy sigh. "I

never meant to uproot unpleasant memories."

Caspar's father dropped his gaze once more and shook his head. "I was a better man then, and not only because I had two proper legs to stand on. When I lost her… Well…" He paused to collect himself. "I did not think I would see Caspar open up to anyone ever again. Yet, for some reason, he has decided to open up to you."

"Your son has a good heart," Keziah replied. "He could have left me to die in the woods. Instead, he brought me here—someone who should have been his enemy—and nursed me back to health. Only a good man would do such a thing, and good men are not grown from spoiled seeds."

"He is good. Too good. He might just be better than the pair of us…" Caspar's father let his shoulders sag, as though finally relenting to years' worth of unacknowledged pain. But that was nothing compared to that which he was about to inflict. "Which is why, if you love him, you must leave."

Keziah's heart stopped. The words cut deeper than any arrow, giving voice to the fears her mind had already concocted. *If you love him…* They carved out the little chink in her heart that had been reserved for him.

…you must leave.

The request, so plain and so innocently given, broke her.

The worst part of the whole situation was that she'd already made up her mind to do just that. If only this conversation had never happened, she could have gone on imagining a future between her and Caspar, even if she returned home. Perhaps she would have even convinced herself later to return under better circumstances. If this idea had resided in her mind alone, the newly romantic side of her could have continued to thrive.

But hearing it from another's mouth was a unique kind

of torture. His father's words removed all doubts from her mind, all fantastical ideas of love as well.

No matter how broken she felt, she held back her tears. They would do her no good here.

"I know…" was all she could muster.

Shadows stretched across the dark lands. A thin whisp of clouds had overtaken the moon.

"Night has fallen heavy enough to provide cover," he added. "I suggest you make haste."

Keziah dipped her head, losing the fight against the waterfall of tears. "I am sorry," she whispered through a tightened throat. She refused to meet his gaze, waiting instead for him to leave before she allowed herself to break.

"As am I," he replied, his voice hinting at genuine sympathy. Caspar's father made to leave, but something stopped him. He waited a heartbeat or two before he called out to her again. "A better man than I might say thank you…"

A bitter cold drew over her shoulders. The final thread of hatred she'd harboured for him snapped.

Though the two of them had been at odds since her arrival, in Caspar they found common ground. Neither had wanted to hurt him or cause trouble, yet, in one way or another, they were the exact reason for his suffering. Without realizing it, they'd simply played out the same generational curses that had plagued these lands for decades.

He was right. They were no better than each other.

As Caspar's father turned back towards the house, she whispered, "A better girl than I might say the same…"

In the absence of the winds, her words carried. Caspar's father said nothing, but the silent pause in his stride said more than enough. He filled his lungs, letting out an audible sigh briefly before hobbling back to the house.

Their moment of honesty hadn't changed his life or hers. At very least, it showed there was a side to him that wasn't bound by the hatreds of their lands—that wasn't conditioned by prejudice. For the first time since their meeting, Keziah found the humanity in him that hurt and time had taken.

When Caspar's father was sufficiently far from earshot, she finally let the tears fall.

🔥CHAPTER 13🌿

ANOTHER CURIOUS NIGHT WITH KEZIAH HAD
left Caspar tossing and turning on the sofa. She'd asked him
the one question he'd actively been avoiding, and she'd done
it so casually, so innocently, that he couldn't even fault her
for the painful memories it brought up.

But he'd lied to her.

Caspar hadn't wanted to lie to her, but he couldn't admit
that he'd thought of leaving many times before. He was too
ashamed of wanting to leave his ailing father, yet he'd
known for a long time that there was nothing here for him.

Not until she'd come along.

Caspar turned again on the sofa, resting his arm over his
eyes as he draped a leg over the backrest.

"Oh, Keziah… What have you done to me?" he
whispered to himself.

Sleep was no easy task either. Every time he closed his
eyes, the only thing he saw was her startled eyes staring back
at him. He'd come so close to both having her and losing

her in the same day. She'd taken his mind, his heart. But he'd given them willingly. Yet, she was the one prize he could not have, the one target he could never reach.

It took him a while to finally fall asleep, and not before considering checking in with Keziah multiple times.

"Caspar!" His father's shout startled him awake.

"Father?" he called back. He leapt from the sofa on instinct alone. His eyes hadn't properly opened, but his heart was already racing. He rushed semi-consciously to his father's room, finding him seated upright on the bed, staring at the window. "Are you okay? Has something happened?"

All rationality had left him. He'd shot into the room without a second thought. The last time his father had woken him up in the middle of the night, he'd been rushed to the doctor. The time before, his mum had died.

The low light of the blue moon filtering in from the window highlighted the lack of sleep on his father's face. Even barely awake, Caspar could tell there was something off about him. He sat too still, too quiet. His usual fire had been ousted, leaving only a sombre cold.

"What's the matter?" Caspar added, rubbing the sleep from his eyes. "Are you hurt?"

His father furrowed his brow. "No, no… I'm fine."

"You don't sound so… Is it your leg? Your heart?"

"No, son," his father replied, unfazed by the concern in his son's tone. He hadn't once glanced at Caspar throughout their interaction. Instead, the window, or what lay beyond, had him transfixed.

Caspar began to wonder if all the old man had wanted was company. He sighed, slumping against the doorframe. The urgency began to subside. He dragged his hands over his face, trying to relieve himself of the worry. "Don't scare me like that," he mumbled between a yawn. "I thought…"

They both knew all too well what he'd thought.

"She loved the night," his father said, as if reading his mind. "Especially nights like these, where the air is cool, dense. She used to say she could practically taste the rain."

"Mother?"

His father nodded. "I never wanted to believe her—I mean, who can taste the rain? Well…" He chuckled softly to himself. "Many a time did she prove me wrong."

Caspar rubbed his eyes. His father had never been one for words. In fact, most of their conversations could be aptly summed up as a series of grunts and nods. It had been a long time since his father had summoned him to simply talk, and longer still since he'd spoken so openly about his mother. Caspar listened attentively, not wishing to ruin the moment with an off-putting question. This brief reflection had stirred something in him, perhaps in them both. It was the closest he'd felt to his father since his mother's death.

"I laugh now, wondering how she must be smiling down on me… As I too can now taste the rain in a drought," he concluded, though his expression was far from jovial, and laughter was miles away.

A tear scurried down his cheek, highlighted by the blue hue of the moon.

A moment like this, so quietly intimate in its torture, threatened to break whatever feeble peace they had established in the household. Conversations surrounding his mother had vanished the day she had. Now, hearing mention of her aloud rattled something old and tender residing within him. That long-ignored grief clawed its way out of hiding and nestled itself into his chest. His throat grew raw, smothering questions that came not from the man he was, but from the little boy who'd lost his mother too soon. His breaths were short, soft. Stifled out of fear that, had his father caught wind of his suffering, the conversation would end, permanently.

Caspar bit down on the questions that begged to be voiced, all the while, the little boy inside him screamed. He laced his arms over his torso, as if giving himself the hug they both needed.

His father pulled his gaze from the window, no longer able to face the light of the moon. His voice was soft, almost pleasing as he spoke.

"I see it now, my boy. Perhaps I'd seen it the whole time, just like the rain…"

"What do you mean?" Caspar replied, his words strained and throat hoarse. The hallmarks of pain so closely resembled a lack of sleep, but his stray tears did not belong to drowsiness.

The silence that settled between them was laden with a palpable guilt. The look in his father's eyes concerned him. It was a look Caspar himself had used in his youth after having broken things he was never meant to touch.

"There is fire in her. She is abrasive and hard-headed, but there is tenderness, too. And in that, I cannot fault you for your attraction. We are more alike than I realised."

Caspar didn't dare speak, lest his words betray his heart.

His father gestured to an aged portrait beside him on the bed. The crumpled parchment had gone through so many foldings and unfoldings that it resembled the cracked clay of the canyons. The ink, slightly faded from the constant bending, traced the outline of the woman that his mind had chosen to forget.

Caspar's hand hovered over it tentatively. It had been

time since he'd seen her. In his memories, she'd taken on the qualities of a ghost. Ethereal, translucent, and faceless.

Seeing the portrait now forced her out of the shadows of his mind.

She was beautiful. Long black hair and heavy brows. Wide, doe-like eyes. Ample bosom. Kind smile. Surprisingly, she shared more than a passing resemblance to Keziah at the age of the drawing.

That's when it clicked. His father's hatred, his sudden mood swings, his nasty comments… And, looking back, his mother's fondness for plants, their reclusive housing…

His mother was *Harri*.

"It is in your nature," his father said, watching him struggle to take hold of the portrait. "She was from a faraway village on the outskirts of Idune. We were never supposed to meet, let alone fall in love." He let out a sigh that seemed decades in the making. "We went through so much pain… I didn't want the same for you."

"Why now?" Caspar replied, retracting his hand from the portrait. He let it fall in a fist at his side as the tears began to roll over his cheeks.

"I thought I was doing what was best for you, my son," he replied softly, using those words as if they would gain him sympathy. As if tugging at the feeble bondage of parenthood whose ropes he'd scarcely tested and wondered if whose knots would hold.

They didn't.

Those same knots had been cast off the moment he'd met Keziah. Unbeknownst to him, she'd been the catalyst for a radical and much needed change in his life. What little time he'd spent with her had proven there existed tethers stronger than those of birth. Tethers that transcended lifetimes.

Tethers made of such threads only fate could see and spin.

Those words garnered no sympathy at all. Instead, they were drowned out by the nervous beating in Caspar's chest. Something was wrong. Very wrong.

"What did you do?!" The words fell from him in a broken snarl—that of a wounded animal on high alert.

"It's your Keziah…" His father hesitated, his voice choking up. "They've taken her."

His hearing faltered

His breath hitched.

His fists trembled.

His heart stopped.

In a single beat, the house turned into a cell, the village to a cage. Part of him wished to claw at the very walls that imprisoned him, to howl in pain until his lungs gave out.

He was a wounded animal, though his pain did not stem from the gash on his foot. It came from the part of him that had been so unscrupulously carved out by those words. A part of him that, 'til now, he'd believed was his and his alone. It wasn't. It had never been. It belonged to her—not by claim or conquer, but by something deeper, more profound. It was a space his heart had reserved for her. One that had existed even before they'd met.

One that had been hers all along.

* * *

Keziah wept in silence, mourning the loss of a life that had never truly been hers. The brief but enduring moments they'd shared brought about a crushing realization. She'd fallen for a man she could never have.

He was powerless, a peasant, and an *Argia* on top of it

144

all. Yet, having gotten to know him, she realised that none of those labels mattered nearly as much as what she felt inside.

But the realisation had come too late.

Cursed Iturri, she thought, for it had brought her the one thing she'd truly wanted, only to unceremoniously strip it from her just as she realised what a gift she'd been given.

But then, they were never meant to meet.

"Stop it, Keziah," she told herself. "You're better than this."

She wiped away the tears and straightened her back. This helplessness which had taken up root in her heart would not win out.

Keziah had never been one to cry over a boy, and Iturri be damned if she was about to start. She knew she would never get over the way Caspar, in the brief time they'd known each other, had made her feel. But she couldn't linger any longer on what might have been. Such things would only keep her stagnant. This place and these people were never hers. Especially not him.

It was time to return to real life.

With a heavy heart, Keziah glanced around the garden, knowing this look would be her last. The soil had been mostly tilled, the paths marked but not lined, and the rows for crops waited to be tended. The garden tools were scattered about the floor—where they'd left them before their escapade. Seeing them was enough to send shivers down her spine.

They'd abandoned their barriers, falling into the throws of passion. But passion spat them back out the other end worse for wear. Ruined by desires the world would never permit and memories they could never claim.

The sight of the unfinished state of things gave her pause. Before they'd tossed away their prejudices in favour of fanning flames, Keziah had innocently wished to help in exchange for Caspar's kindness. Knowing how much the garden had meant to him and his mother, she'd wanted to return it to its state of former glory. It was her gift to him for having saved her life—in more ways than one.

Her teeth danced over the edge of her lip as she contemplated it. Caution suggested she make haste in her departure, but her feet were rooted to the spot. Her desire to help had not faded. Instead, a spark reignited in her heart.

Keziah knew she would always remember Caspar, but she wanted to make sure he never forgot her. A mischievous smile spread across her tear-stained cheeks.

If she was going to leave, she would at least leave a lasting impression.

Keziah clapped her hands together and grounded her feet. Noise be damned, she started fixing the basin beneath the stream.

She cast aside the loose sediment with a flick of her wrist, sending it whizzing through the air towards the mostly tilled garden beds. It would provide the perfect blend of nutrients for the crops Caspar intended to plant.

Wafts of the surrounding lavender plants curled around her as she moved. Warmth spread over her shoulders. It felt like a hug from her ancestors.

Keziah took it as a sign she was doing the right thing.

Sweat began to pool at her brow. It had been a while since she'd exerted herself in this way. Yet, using her powers turned that spark in her to flame. Her lungs burned with the strain of the moves, but she welcomed the sensation. It reminded her of her strength.

Next, Keziah thrust her hands up in front of her, pulling up some of the larger stones residing deep within the soil. The ground grumbled at first but soon gave in to her will. These stones lined the basin, slowing the seeping of the water into the tender soils below. Slowly but surely, the basin began to fill.

The sound of the trickling water hitting the stone reminded her of the pitter patter of rain on her forest home—a sound Keziah had unconsciously longed for since her arrival. It was yet another sign that it was time to return. And she would, without complaint, once she was finished with Caspar's surprise.

With another flourish, she attacked the canyon wall, pulling forward part of the face to provide privacy.

Keziah stepped back to admire her own handiwork. The area looked nothing like the place Caspar had shown her when she'd first arrived. It had been completely and utterly transformed, becoming a quiet corner of natural luxury, rather than the squatting peasant's stream in which he'd made her bathe. It was beautiful, natural, and kept all the conservative charm of the original, "unbroken" washing station.

Suddenly, the sound of feet appeared around her. They weren't the soft, hesitant footsteps she'd come to associate with Caspar, nor the off kilter clomp of his father. Three sets of feet to be precise. Three sets that sent the hairs on the back of her neck reaching towards the rising moon.

"Who's there?" she hissed. The call garnered no reply, but the footsteps grew louder. The scene reminded her eerily of the time she'd met Caspar, but she'd doubted she'd be met with the same hospitality that he'd shown her.

One of the shrubs higher up the canyon wall shifted

suspiciously.

"I am not in the mood for games with peasants who have no idea with whom they are playing," she added, but was swiftly responded to with a barrage of pebbles. "Halt!" When nothing happened, she tacked on a generous, "please." But the attack continued. "I order you…"

The attack grew, hastened by her orders. Whoever it was clearly had no intention of letting up. "Fine," Keziah replied. "I asked nicely."

With one fluid motion, she pulled all the pebbles from the air and swirled them around her body. The vortex the moving stones created cast a light breeze around her, lifting her partially damp hair. She looked like a woman possessed, like the living echo of *Iturri*.

"NOW!" a voice yelled from above.

Suddenly, heavy cords of rope fell upon her. The next thing Keziah knew, she was trapped beneath a net, being battered by the same stones she'd manipulated. How quickly things had turned. It had only taken them a breath, but all of a sudden, she was fighting for hers.

"Let me g—" she began to scream.

A rock struck, interrupting her plea. The side of her head throbbed momentarily before she began to lose consciousness. The words slipped away. She struggled only seconds longer before relenting to the swift embrace of the concussion. With what little consciousness she had left, she felt the group of people hoist her up and carry her off. A solitary tear slid down her cheek as she wished for someone to come save her. But who would ever save a *Harri* here?

"Caspar…" she whispered, before the darkness finally claimed her.

⚜ CHAPTER 14 ⚜

GONE…

Caspar stared breathlessly at the newly remodelled bathing house he could only attribute to her. But Keziah was nowhere to be found.

Anger gurgled away in the pit of his stomach. Though not an angry person by nature, Caspar found himself spiralling into the depths of it. He wondered how long it must have resided in him to consume him so completely. He'd tortured himself mercilessly on their way back from the beach because he'd convinced himself they would never work. Yet, he'd raced out in a panic to find her, the woman he'd never meant to meet and might never see again.

Rage took the place of his sorrows. Part of it belonged to his father and the impotence he'd used as a crutch ever since his mother died. Part of it was unjustly directed at his mother for having left them too soon. Some of it was reserved for the villagers and their stupid feud. Some for Keziah, who'd pulled the arrow from his heart—where he'd stuck it—and made it beat again.

But the lion's share of this rage was riddled with guilt and belonged to him alone. For allowing himself to live in this trap for so long. For not leaving sooner. For his prejudices. And most importantly, for losing something he'd so desperately desired without even the chance to fight for it.

For it was true; she'd been taken.

Footprints trailed across the dirt, and not just one pair, many. The tell-tale signs of struggle were all present. Fallen stones. Drag marks. Agitated dust. There had been a fight, or at least the makings of one.

Caspar swore at the ground as he slammed a fist into the wall. The heat of impending tears stung in the backs of his eyes. The longer he looked, the more agitated he became. She hadn't just been taken—she'd been ambushed.

He knew the only people capable of such cruelty were the soldiers they'd passed. Perhaps they hadn't been careful enough after all with Keziah's disguises. All they'd needed was an excuse to let their hatred take charge.

If they wanted hatred, Caspar would gladly oblige.

Without a second thought, he made haste back up to the house. Ignoring his stuttering father, he grabbed his bow and arrows and raced out into the dead of night. The hunter in him surfaced, losing no time in tracking down the panicked footprints.

The moon above shone bright, wide-eyed and watchful. The usual nighttime bluster was nowhere to be found, shifting no sands, stifling no sounds. The trail would be easy enough to follow. Caspar just hoped he wasn't already too late.

Sweat pooled in his palms. The wound on his foot

reopened, blood blooming beneath the bandages. Still, nothing would deter him.

He'd made the mistake of giving her up once. If he wasn't quick about it, he might lose her in a way that could never be undone.

* * *

When Keziah came to, she was immediately ambushed with the scent of salt and a noise that reverberated around her like thunder. It roared unpleasantly, ringing loudly in her already aching head.

"Release me," she said woozily, hardly hearing her own voice over the sound. "Release me at once," she tried again, throwing more force into the words despite her grave disorientation. When no response came, Keziah tried her best to open her eyes. Her vision was still blurred from the conk to her head, but she could make out various figures surrounding her. They shuffled along on all sides of her, carrying her somewhere, and ignoring her pleas in the process.

How dare…

Suddenly her heart picked up the pace, as if shocking her back to reality. The next roar came as a jolt to her system, a bolt of lightning right down her spine. She recognised this roar, this wicked sound. She realised she was surrounded, not only by people, but by her worst nightmare: the ocean.

Keziah thrashed her arms about, hoping to find something to grab hold of, but the tight cords of a net prevented her escape. They dug into her skin as she tried in vain to right herself.

"Let me go!" she yelled, kicking and flailing about against the many hands that carried her closer and closer to her doom.

"Quiet, you soil leech!" screamed one of the boys.

"This will teach you to come into our lands, you unwelcome swine," said another.

Keziah squirmed harder, but their calloused hands gripped tighter. "How dare you speak to me—" she began but froze as she noticed the dreaded pull of the current beneath her. "Stop!" she begged as fear flooded her system, removing all pretence of the hardened upper-class maiden she'd wished to portray. "Please!" she cried, her sobs rattling around the cave, getting lost in the echoes of the waves.

It was no use. The cold of the water seeping into her clothes was a bitter reminder of death's willing embrace, slow and unrelenting, and deaf to any pleas of salvation.

Her next cry for help was muffled by her sudden plunge into the depths. They'd tossed her into the churning tides, still caught like a fish in the net, unable to free herself, let alone move. But it wouldn't have mattered. Keziah was still unable to swim.

Water rushed into her lungs. She couldn't move. She couldn't breathe. Like every other stone she'd known, she sank, and this time, there was no one there to catch her.

* * *

The bitter cold of the night did nothing to quell the fire raging within him. Caspar's lungs burned with the dryness of the desert air. Each breath was a shower of glass, but despite the pain, he knew he could not relent. He ran as fast as he could, ignoring the shooting pain in his foot and chest. His heart pounded heavily, as if trying to outpace his legs— as though his own life depended on it.

The incautious footprints led back to the cave from earlier that day. A sinking feeling told him the attackers were not there for a pleasant swim.

"Keziah!" he screamed into the tunnel. His feet did not hesitate in waiting for a response. They charged into the cave—into the dark, prodded on by a fear much greater than that of his own survival.

The looming sense of dread followed. The roar of the ocean beyond beckoned him forward and curdled his blood. Caspar hoped to hear some sign of Keziah in the echo of the waves. Instead, he heard only the mocking of the tides.

The tunnel was no longer his friend. Now, it stood between him and her—as had everything and everyone else since their first encounter.

Suddenly, the sound of laughter met his ears. Caspar froze as a group of village boys appeared from deeper inside the tunnel. He'd been right all along. They were the same soldiers that had been jeering from atop the canyons. Five of them. Three around his age, one that looked too old to be hanging around with them, and a final younger one who struggled to keep up. As their eyes, gleaming with pride and violence, met his, they came to a halt.

The boys spread out across the width of the cave, forming a sinister sort of barricade. Their grins hinted at malice and triumph. Caspar's blood turned to ice.

"What have you done to her?" Caspar's voice was barely more than a hiss, his teeth grinding together as he marched toward the nearest boy. This one was around his age, but the knowingly defiant curl of his lip spoke of aged hatred.

He grabbed hold of the boy's tunic and slammed him against the wall. The thud was masked by the sound of a heavy breaking wave, but he could feel the boy's breath leave his chest. He threw all his weight into the stance, his fingers tightening around the fabric of the collar. The boy struggled beneath his noose-like grip, searching for the air that had been knocked out of him.

"What do you care," the boy spat. "She was a savage…" The boy's eyes glinted with malice. "Just like you."

Caspar had no clue what came over him in that moment. It was as though he'd left his body and allowed something else to take hold—the wounded animal within.

A clenched fist flew into the boy's jaw. And another, and another. Blood trickled from the boy's mouth, covering Caspar's knuckles entirely. The others jumped in to save him, but Caspar was too quick. He tossed the first boy to the ground before whipping an arrow from his quiver.

"Calm down," said the older boy.

As if anything could quell the rage in his soul. Caspar no longer saw the boys—he saw creatures. Demons. Targets.

He nocked his arrow and pointed it at each of the boys as they moved. His eyes glazed over with hatred. These people, his people, had done something so vile, so unforgivable, that he scarcely considered them worthy of life. Their prejudices had gotten the best of them, and it was Keziah's poor soul to pay.

"You should be ashamed of yourself," growled one of the boys as he tiptoed tentatively around Caspar's arrowhead. "Sticking up for an animal—"

"The only animals here are you," Caspar hissed in reply.

The seconds ticked by relentlessly, but neither party made to move. Despite his hatred, Caspar was unable to fire. Unable to take the life of another, even one so deserving of suffering. The boy, in turn, could not fight back.

But this was the nature of war. In battles of hatred, none prevail.

"*Yallah*. Let's get out of here," the boy finally called out.

His voice quivered; his conviction had wavered now that they were at the mercy of another. "Leave this traitor to himself…"

All but one of the boys filed out of the cave, muttering words that would've earned them punishments elsewhere. The youngest of the group, barely marked by the sun, chin hardly shadowed by maturity, remained. He'd avoided the initial scuffle, clinging close to the outer wall of the cave. He looked from the group to Caspar with tears in his eyes, as if his next move would mark him forever.

"I didn't mean for—"

"Where. Is. She."

"Deep," he gulped. The boy's voice was little more than a whimper, but he seemed to have come to his decision. "She's in the deep…" he clarified, grabbing Caspar by the elbow and guiding him into the cave.

The crashing sounds of the waves echoed wildly around them. The tide had come in with a fury. Even the best of swimmers would have problems traversing the currents.

Caspar stripped off his robes and dove in. He couldn't think about the thrashing of the waves. He couldn't think about the burning of the salt in his wound. He couldn't think of the urchins or sharp rocks beneath him. All he could think about was her.

The other boy followed, appearing beside him through the sea foam. The boy did not appear to be a strong swimmer, but he would not heed Caspar's words to go back. He looked determined to help fix the mess he'd made. Caspar couldn't waste more time on him. If he was willing to risk his life, that was his choice. Time was running out and Keziah was still nowhere to be found.

From beneath the surface, the menacing sounds from

above were silenced. The current dragged pebbles across the seabed, but even those sounds were muffled by the ominously dark waters. Beneath the waves, life halted, as though a preview to whatever came after. Even in his frantic search, Caspar was not immune to the cold creeping into his heart. It ate at his bones, as did the urgency.

But he could not give up.

The currents fought to drag him down to the depths of the chasm as he scanned the seabed. His muscles and chest burned, but he could not stop. The churned-up waters had lifted the sands from the floor, limiting visibility.

When he could hold his breath no longer, Caspar surfaced. He cast a glance around the agitated pool, looking for signs of the other boy. The currents had him fighting to tread water.

Suddenly, the boy broke the surface. "She's over there!" he called over the roar of the waves as he pointed to the edge of the cavern.

Caspar followed his direction to the mouth of the cave that led out to the open ocean. He took a deep breath and dove down as far as he could. The boy was right. Keziah's body drifted dangerously close to the chasm. It waited hungrily for her to be swept in with the next wave and tossed out to sea.

His world ground to a halt as he laid eyes on her.

Keziah's body hung, suspended in the depths like a discarded puppet. She'd lost consciousness. Her arms floated out at her sides as though tied to invisible strings. Her ebony hair a dark halo against the eerie blue of the deep. Her dress billowed at her hips, dancing with the ripples of the currents.

She drifted along, a suspended angel in the dark. Bubbles

clung to her, shimmering under the glow of whatever dim light managed to break through to the depths. She sparkled, as though lit up by the stars that so fascinated her on land. The rest of her was still. Docile. Her face was pale, lips slightly parted. Her expression was unnervingly serene—as though she were sleeping.

But the tides were ruthless, and she was entirely at their mercy.

Caspar lunged for her waist, dragging her up from the dark. He kicked frantically, struggling with her weight as well as his own, but the little boy came up beside him just in time. They broke through the surface together, Keziah hanging limply between them.

As they paddled back to shore, Caspar prayed to all the stars he'd ever seen to bring her back. He hoisted Keziah's body out of the water in one fell swoop.

His muscles screamed in protest, but Caspar refused to stop until he knew she was safe. The pebbles dug into his feet, into his wound. He swayed, heavy and unsteady, but prodded onward, far from the tide that had nearly stolen her away.

The blue of the sea clung to Keziah's skin, its cold sapping the warmth from her body. Her dress hung heavy over his arms as a cascade of water fell from it. Step by step, Caspar made for higher ground, whisking her as far away from the sea as possible. The boy followed closely behind, panting as he dropped to the floor beside them.

As Caspar lay her body down, he looked over at the boy, whose expression had darkened at being confronted with the horrible truth of his actions.

"Will she make it?" the boy asked, his voice barely a whisper over the sound of the waves.

Caspar's throat tightened as he pressed his ear against her sternum. The world fell silent except for the pounding of his own heart in his ears. He waited. Listened.

Nothing.

"She's not breathing…" he mumbled to himself, his own breath coming in short, panicked bursts. He ignored the boy's question, not out of anger or resentment, but because he had no answer—or at least, not one which he was yet willing to accept.

"You… You have to help her," said the boy, reaching over to prop her head into position. "You have to breathe for her."

Caspar hadn't done such a thing before, and he had no idea how the boy knew what to do—or if it would even work—but he had no time to question.

If I have never asked for one favour, Iturri, I beg of you this one… save this woman… he repeated to himself.

Caspar cupped her jaw in his hands and took a deep breath before sealing his mouth over hers. Her lips were cold and unresponsive to his touch. His heart raced, but hers was silent.

At another time, in another place, he might have been over the moon at the intimate act. He'd wished for as much only the night before. But now, all he could think about was how he may never get the chance.

He breathed into her, willing life back into her body. Her chest barely rose. He tried again, fighting the ache in his own lungs.

Still nothing.

"Put force on her chest," the boy said, touching his own chest in demonstration. His voice wavered, but there was an urgency behind it. "And press hard."

Caspar looked up at him questioningly, a mixture of sweat and seawater dripping from his brow. He hesitated only a second, fearing he might hurt her, but time was of the essence. He cupped his hands over her chest and began pumping them, imitating the beat of her heart.

Come on…

He pressed his lips against her mouth again, forcing the air into her lungs, begging her release from the grip of death.

Please…

Caspar's fingers trembled as he pressed harder. He gritted his teeth. She still wasn't responding. "Come back to me…" he whispered to her as tears streamed down his cheeks. "Please."

Nothing since his mother's death had hurt this much. When she'd died, Caspar had thought she'd taken all his tears with her. But Keziah had somehow found them, brought them back. He could not lose her, too.

He leaned over her again, readying himself with another life-giving breath. His hope dwindled, but he would not say goodbye. Not like this. He was about to resume pressure when a weak, strangled sound appeared at her lips. He froze.

"Keziah…?"

Finally, she coughed. The sound caught him so off guard that it almost sent him toppling backwards. Relief flooded his heart. The shadows receded from her body. The nervous tension that had built up in him snapped, sending shivers down his spine.

The sea had released her.

Caspar wasted no time as he guided her onto her side, supporting her as she heaved up mouthfuls of seawater. Her body shuddered violently, and her breathing was ragged, but at least she was breathing. Keziah heaved until there was nothing left in her. Her skin was still clammy and cold, but it had finally regained a semblance of its original colour.

"Caspar…" she breathed. Her voice was hoarse and uneven, but the sound of it alone was akin to a choir of angels.

He pulled her in close, pressing her against his chest to keep her warm.

"You're safe," he whispered into the crown of her head. "I've got you."

"Is she okay?" came a soft murmur. The little boy sat opposite them, watching with tears in his eyes. "I'm so sorry," he whispered. "I don't even know why I followed them…"

Caspar nodded, though he feared the memory of such trauma would stay with her forever. He didn't know how he would even begin to help her heal something like this. And who was to stop those boys from trying a stunt like this again?

"Come on," he said finally as he cradled a resting Keziah in his arms. "There's no use in us waiting around."

His father was right. She didn't belong here. It would've been better for both of them if they'd never met.

By the time they exited the tunnel, Caspar had already made up his mind. She wouldn't be happy about it, but at least she would be safe.

❦ CHAPTER 15 ❦

"PLEASE…"

The sound of the waves grew, echoing in the back of her semiconscious mind like the growling of a hungry wolf. Open your eyes, Keziah, she thought. Open your eyes before it's too late.

"Don't…"

They had hunted her like the most astute of wolves. They came in a pack, growling and snarling as good as any beast. Their laughs, laced with malice that did not belong to them, but rather their forefathers. Animals, she thought. And yet, they called her the same.

"I can't…"

A rush of cold grazed her back. Her dress grew heavy in their hands. The fabric swelled, pulling taut against the upper part of her body as the water climbed its fibres. Her fighter's spirit kicked in, pulling her out of her daze. She kicked and flailed her arms about, straining against the net around her. She was trapped, a fish caught and primed for slaughter.

"…breathe."

Keziah was startled awake by the sound of a heavy door

slamming shut. She wiped the cold sweat from her brow as she propped herself up on the pillows. The familiar scents of lavender and pine danced around her, but they didn't comfort her as they once used to.

The nightmare had ended, yet it seemed a new one was just beginning.

Was it all a dream? she wondered, fighting against the sleep still lingering in her mind.

Keziah rubbed her eyes and frowned at the draping colours hanging over her canopy bed. She was alone, a cup of blueberry leaf tea growing cold beside her. The morning light filtered in through the patchwork canopy outside her window. Birds chirped in the distance. The slow settling mists danced between the tree trunks. Her eyes widened as she took in the vast forest that extended far beyond her wooden walls.

Mornings like these would have been a blessing to a past version of her. They would've meant stealing away from her family and exploring the forest, practicing her powers in secret, and wishing for adventure at the line where the earth runs dry.

After everything that had happened, her peace had turned from green leaves and misty seas to red rocks and open desert skies.

And him.

But somehow, she'd returned home. She was back in her bedroom, wrapped in her favourite flower-embroidered quilt. She peeked beneath the blanket. Someone had stripped her of her white linens and clothed her in her red silk sleeping gown.

No…

A gilded mirror hung on the wall opposite, reflecting the

waking image of the daughter of the borderland chief. The room was every bit as regal as she'd left it. It was as though nothing had ever happened, as if she'd never left home. Yet, everything had changed.

Keziah leapt from the bed. Her heart raced. She shouldn't be back… She couldn't be… She whipped open the door of her room to the plant-lined courtyard. The wooden floors shook beneath her heavy steps.

No… Tears began to form at the corners of her eyes.

Racing down the wraparound porch towards the main hall, her long black hair fluttered behind her like a cape. Why was she back in her village? The last thing she remembered was the tug of the deep as she sank below the waves. A shiver passed over her at the memory.

The morning air was damp and cool, still clinging to the nightly rains. In spite of this, sweat formed at her brow. Fear lingered from the experience, even now, even on land. Images of the attack came in sudden flashes—each corner, each shadow causing her to doubt her surroundings. Where she once sought renewal in this morning petrichor, she now found only the sharp reminder of the waves. Keziah shook off another of those horrible memories as she passed the next hall.

She'd come back. Back to the village and back to life. But at what cost?

Keziah rounded the next corner and threw open the doors to the main hall of the house, only to find it empty. Her family and their servants were nowhere to be seen. The echo of her footsteps slowly dissipated around her as she stared at the expectant furniture.

Her heart fell in her chest, consumed by a sickening cocktail of guilt, confusion, and urgency. Keziah forced the air back into her lungs from the run, each huff sending out visible plumes of hot air into the vacant space. Someone needed to explain this wicked turn of events to her, now. She was about to yell for help when she noticed a trickle of smoke from outside the window.

Something was going on at the village main hall. The smoke was a signal to the rest of the village to gather. They tinged it different colours using leaves and petals from the forest. Depending on the topic of the hearing, these petals were added to the flames to alert the village beforehand. Blue smoke meant teaching or knowledge sharing. Green smoke meant healing. White smoke meant marriage. Red smoke meant danger…

But this smoke tinged the morning sky black, and black smoke meant only one thing.

Death.

But who could possibly be on trial?

Suddenly, her heart stopped.

Caspar wouldn't have brought me here himself… would he?

Without a second thought, Keziah burst from the house and rushed towards the main hall, hoping she wasn't too late. Family or not, she wouldn't let them get away with this. If they did have Caspar holed up in there, she'd overturn the very earth the hall stood on before she let them harm a single hair on his head.

The sound of the door whipping open startled the occupants of the room. Every head in the chamber snapped towards her.

Inside, the air was thick with the scent of woodsmoke and ash. A stifling heat emanated from the fire at the centre of the room. It crackled away in a stone basin that had been there longer than the town itself. Dreaded plumes of black smoke billowed upwards into the sky through an opening in the ceiling, blotting out the usual trickle of sunlight which the canopies allowed onto their forest floors.

These flames flickered hungrily, casting shadows across the faces of all present. There, beneath the high, vaulted ceiling, her father sat on his raised cushion conversing with men whose faces she recognized but whose titles she'd always ignored. Time had carved marks of pressure, war, and weighted decisions in his rich brown skin. Such stress had added the salt to his peppercorn hair. It had also added the muscles to his torso and bite to his words. His green eyes were as cold as any frost-coated leaf, and as they stared her down, she felt the same bite of winter in his judging gaze.

Once upon a time, those eyes were kinder, that gaze softer. But since she'd begun to grow out of the doll-like persona he'd attributed to her, carving her own path through life, his kindness turned into caution. Like her, he was stubborn. Immovable. So firm in his convictions that, once made, he never wavered.

This is what it meant to be chief of a border town—especially one with the *Argia*. Fire and earth were at constant odds, and he was the first line of defence. His word was law—a quality he'd brought into their homelife as well.

Upon hearing the ruckus, he turned, his expression impassive as his cold eyes met hers. As they bounced over her person, they reflected this battle as though he were deciding on how to address her—as the little girl he'd doted upon, or the woman who'd shunned his way of life. Keziah knew better than to seek out compassion in his gaze, and better still than to show any desire for it.

"You're awake," he said, his voice as harsh as a winter

breeze. He'd chosen his side. She knew she'd have to be even more forceful in hers.

"Where is he, Father?" Keziah hissed in reply.

A scowl appeared on his face, one that rattled her very bones, but she would not be deterred. If this black smoke meant what she thought it did, Caspar's life was hanging somewhere in the balance, ready to be made an example of.

"Father, I will repeat myself only once. Where is he?" When no answer came, she stomped towards the firepit, threatening to overturn the lot. "You will not harm a hair on his head, or I will burn this village to the ground."

"Is that how you would greet your family after such an ordeal?" he asked, his eyes narrowing at her as he waved away his company. "One would think you would be grateful to be back in your own home."

"Father, he is my friend—" she began, but her response was quickly met with a sharp crack that made the words catch in her throat.

He rose from his cushion, the splintered wooden staff in hand. The pent-up pressure in his palm had snapped it in two.

"Friendship… with an *Argia*?!" Her father laughed, but there was no happiness in it. It was a harsh reminder of his hatred. "What a foolish notion, even for you. A scrawny mouse like that could never be your friend. That is delusion and disrespect, neither of which I will stand for, and least of all from my daughter."

His voice echoed throughout the sparsely decorated chamber. Not even the ornate tapestries lining the walls could dampen the sound. At this point, most of the occupants had fled the room. The few who remained maintained a personal interest in the conversation.

Two similar looking young men flanked her father. The ties of blood held fast to them, apparent in the strong cut of their jaws and lime green eyes—her brothers. Her eldest brother leaned against one of the beams with his arms crossed over his torso, disappointment highlighting his gaze. Her other brother watched from closer, a subtle smirk on his face. Family yes, but not the kind she'd look to for kindness or sympathy. Her brothers had always been happy to see her, the baby of the family, suffer the consequences of her actions, merited or not.

Off to the side, her Tante waited, twirling a stray lock of her long, peppered braid. Though she might have sympathised with Keziah on other occasions, she rarely went against her brother, Keziah's father.

She was on her own in a den of wolves.

Keziah had no interest in making a spectacle of their argument, but she could tell her father had other plans.

"Father, he is not an enemy," she replied, tempering her anger.

"Do you hear yourself?" He furrowed his brow. "They have warped your mind. To make friends with such a creature…" Each word felt like a dagger to her heart. He had no idea what she'd been through with Caspar, and yet he stood spouting the same harmful rhetoric as always. The same sentiment that burned through him lingered in Caspar's father, too. "You have forgotten your place?"

Though fear rose up in her, Keziah did not retreat. She met her father's stubbornness with her own. He'd always taught her to be strong, to fight for what she believed in, and to not tolerate ignorance. Well, she'd return the favour of the lesson.

She clenched her fists at her sides. "To be your rose in

an iron cage?" she hissed through gritted teeth.

"Keziah, this is not up for debate!" Her father's temper exploded, his anger rattling the heavy rafters above their heads. Her brothers took a step back. Her Tante hid her face. "His very eyes burn the colour of destruction—of war. He may be no *kanala,* but he came armed all the same. You would still claim him to be innocent?"

"Was it not him to bring me home?" she countered. The flames of loyalty rose inside her—not for the lands that bore her, rather for the boy who'd freed her.

"After stealing you away in the first place." Her father stalked towards her, his hefty figure blocking the view of the others.

"He helped me," Keziah whispered, recoiling slightly at his approach. Her heart trembled. He towered over her, looking down upon her with reckoning in his eyes.

"He injured you..." her father replied, scowling at the bandage on her arm. "Plucked you from your home, stole you from your family, threatened to—"

"I left!" The words burst from her lips before she could stop them, as though her heart had decided to scream where her mind could barely whisper. But she was not about to let Caspar be blamed for something he didn't do.

She'd been the one to leave the "safety" of her home. She'd wanted to practice her powers, to learn to stand up for herself with more than just words. She wished to be more than a simple wife or token heir. But that was never part of her father's agenda.

The room suddenly fell quiet. Even the sound of the crackling fire seemed to catch itself, as though waiting.

Keziah knew her words were a mistake as soon as they'd left her lips. The shadows of the flames licked his person, highlighting the rage in his eyes. In them, she spied a flicker of instability, uncertainty. It was a look so foreign to her that he no longer looked like her father. He looked almost like the villains in his stories.

"Father…" she breathed. Her throat was too tight, her heart too fearful to properly speak. But it was trigger enough.

Her father snapped. With one hefty swing, she felt the sting of his calloused hand on her cheek. The sharp sound echoed, etched into her mind long after the strike. The rest of her family stifled gasps.

Keziah was left dazed and dumbfounded.

The force sent her staggering back a step. A dull ringing appeared in her left ear as her vision began to blur. The mark burned hot on her cheek long after his hand pulled away. Shock and anger fell in uncontrolled tears down the sides of her face, but Keziah kept silent. She reached trembling fingers up to the red and swelling side of her face, struggling to comprehend what had just taken place.

He'd never struck her before.

Her father let out a tempered growl, one cloaked with hatred but stitched with vulnerability. "You embarrassed our tribe. You let an *Argia* fool take advantage of our weakness. You have disgraced my name and that of our family. I will not hear another word about that creature. Not now, not ever."

"Brother…" called her Tante from behind. Her voice trembled in the wake of the slap. "That's enough. She's just a child…"

"A child who threatened our village with destruction."

His words dislodged the last shred of unquestioning loyalty she felt to him. Father or not, his actions went against all of his previous teachings. Fear had overridden his humanity. In the end, Keziah realized he was just as broken and biased as the people of Caspar's lands—the people he claimed to despise most in the world.

"If what you seek is the image of destruction, Father, I shall fetch you a mirror," Keziah said, her voice hoarse as it fought against a tightened throat and tear-stained eyes.

Her father's eyes widened with rage. His fists trembled at his sides, as though ready to unleash another strike. The basin beside them shook, though it wasn't clear whose energy was threatening its rupture.

"I will hear no more. If this whole escapade was to prove to me you are strong enough on your own, you are mistaken. I have been too lenient with you. You have come back, by the grace of Iturri, to our village relatively unharmed, but you would be wrong to think I will ever let you out of this place again. Sister, take her from my sight…"

Before Keziah could argue, her Tante rushed to her side and tugged her away from her father.

"Come child," she said, her voice soft but stern. "It is neither the place nor the time…"

"But—"

"You have spoken your piece. There is nothing more to do." As her Tante pulled her towards the exit, she whispered in Keziah's ear. "Know when you must retreat. Let those words germinate in his mind, for now."

"But Tante…" Keziah whispered in reply. "I think I love him…"

Her Tante's steps faltered only a second. There was no telling what other emotions hid behind those concerned eyes of hers, but her gaze darkened. Her hand closed tighter around Keziah's arm as if to keep her quiet, compliant. She tugged her around the corner and off to the bathing house, far from her father's rage.

All the while, Keziah bit down on the tears welling up in her eyes, knowing that not only had the image of family she'd upheld in her mind shatter, but the respect for her traditions had, too.

❦ CHAPTER 16 ❦

THE BATHHOUSE LAY AT THE OPPOSITE END of the courtyard, screened in by multiple sliding doors. It was reinforced with granite pillars as thick as tree trunks. The ceiling was left open to the forest canopy to allow rainwater into the tubs. These tubs, pools made of the same granite, glittered when wet and hit with the occasional beams of sunlight.

Vines with wide leaves climbed from the slats in the wooden floors, reaching for the skies. Bitter ginger lilies swayed in the morning breeze. Blossom-shaped soap bars lined the walls, along with vials of scented salts and oils. The fragrances seeped from the room, reaching far beyond the confines of the bathhouse.

Keziah sat in a prepared tub, surrounded by curls of steam and the lavender suds she'd once loved. The sound of a crackling fire filled the otherwise silent air, the flames warming a pot of smooth river rocks used to adjust the temperature of the water. She toyed with the few that lay at the bottom of the bath, enjoying the burn on the soles of her feet.

Her Tante had stripped her of the silken nightgown and ushered her into the bath without pity. She was a hard woman, born of soil and sorrow—more even than the stories she'd told Keziah of injuries and broken hearts. She had no children of her own and thus devoted her every waking hour to Keziah and her brothers, treating them like the little ones she never had. She was the only person Keziah had ever truly respected in the village.

She had been her only confidant—her only friend.

But the silence had settled heavy between them. Keziah felt betrayed by her, not for having allowed her father's strike, but for not sticking up for her in the wake of it—where it really mattered. They hadn't spoken since she'd uttered those fateful words that haunted her thoughts even now.

I think I love him…

In the aftermath of their fight, her Tante set about scrubbing off the stubborn layer of red dust that still clung to her skin and wound. Instead of conversation, the repeated sound of the cloth dunking in the water and dragging across her skin filled the silence. With each splash, the overwhelming scent of lavender danced around them.

In what felt like a previous life—the one before Caspar—this scent brought about sensations of peace. Now, it brought only pain. This scent she'd long associated with her Tante and their chatting sessions had found new associations, a boy, a stream, and a sky full of stars.

Her Tante ran an ivory comb through her glistening ebony locks. Her stiff fingers gently worked the strands of hair, removing the tangles with care. At some point, when the silence grew too heavy even for her, she began humming. It was a soft tune, a lullaby, the lyrics of which Keziah knew all too well.

Lover birds on clothing lines,
Turtle dove and swallow,
Sing one low and sing one high,
Their song of hope and sorrow.
Morning blooms and evergreens,
A pain no flame can borrow,
With bitter wind they spread their wings
And hope for home tomorrow.

Normally, this would have been enough to quell even the worst of Keziah's inner storms. But not today. For the first time, the lyrics were more than just words. They spoke to the wars raging within her.

"Tante, it isn't fair…" Keziah whispered as she curled her knees up to her chest. She sat sulking in the warm bath water. Tears began to fall, carving a salty path down her cheeks.

"Your father is doing what he feels is best for the village," her Tante replied. "And for you—"

"But Tante, he doesn't know them. He hasn't even set foot outside these lands."

Her Tante stopped humming. "What makes you think that?"

"He wouldn't be so stubborn if he had…" Keziah sank lower into her knees, the swelling on her cheek still throbbing.

"Hmm…" The comb slowed to a halt at the edge of her hair. "Your father has his reasons for wanting to keep you safe—keep us all safe."

"He is not keeping us safe, Tante. He is keeping us

trapped."

"Is that what you believe?"

Keziah nodded as she closed her eyes, letting her mind drift to the lavender soap in the poor man's bucket beside the stream at Caspar's house. The memory of the heat and dust of the Red Desert sent shivers over her shoulders. She pictured him, wiping the sweat from his brow as he worked away at the garden. The smile on his face as she neared. The way they tumbled around in the dirt.

Somewhere in her own lands, he was being held captive. He'd whisked her away from this cage of a village, showed a world beyond the damp mosses and rich greens, and this was the price they'd both pay for it—her, to be locked away forever, and him, condemned to death. Her heart wept, knowing she was powerless to stop it.

"Do you know what the lyrics of that song speak of, my little kestrel?" her Tante asked as she resumed combing.

"It's a love song…" Keziah grumbled.

"Wrong. It's a song of tragedy, of broken dreams. Two birds of different kinds who were never meant to meet but fell in love anyways, until the winds ripped them apart…"

No wonder it hurts this time, thought Keziah. The lyrics came as another slap to the face, a reminder of the gift she was almost given, as if fate had decided to further irritate her wounds.

"It hurts, does it not?" her Tante prodded.

Her Tante was a woman smarter than most. Nothing she did or said was trivial. Keziah gritted her teeth; the sour taste of the impending lesson hit her tongue before the words ever left her lips.

"You know it does. So, why do you sing it?" Keziah grumbled.

"Why does the wounded wolf cry out to the moon?"

"Tante, I'm not in the mood for another lesson!"

The words left her lips with more bite than she'd intended. In their wake, a heavy silence consumed the air.

"Then," her Tante said finally, rising from her perch beside the bath, "I am not in the mood to help."

"No, wait…" Keziah sniffled. "I apologize. Didn't mean—"

"And that is your problem, child. You see only what is in front of you, and not the story behind it…" Her Tante slid back down onto her perch and began combing again.

Keziah's lip trembled; her eyes held back tears. "Why does the wounded wolf cry out to the moon?" she asked, her voice barely a whisper.

"He cries to be heard, and in his cry, he is remembered," her Tante replied, her voice dripping with gentle maternal victory. "There is a story of a woman of earth who crossed the border and fell in love with a man of fire. Their meeting, though brief, led to months of courting. He would bring her bouquets of lavender and leave them at the edge of the forest. She in turn would leave him little gems from the mines of her people. Soon, the bouquets were accompanied by poems, and she found herself hopelessly besotted with the man's words. This continued through the humid summers and long into the time when the leaves began to change. Eventually, she'd convinced herself she was going to run away to be with him…"

As her Tante wove the tale, Keziah found herself replaying the lyrics over in her head, drifting unconsciously into a memory she'd long forgotten. The song conjured images of the sun peeking through the canopy, leaves glistening with the morning's dew, and little hands clinging to damp bark, climbing as high as they could go…

In her mind, a younger her sat perched on the edge of a tree branch, watching two kestrels build a nest. The scene came back as though it had been only yesterday. The winter had been harsh, but the lively scents of the mosses and flowers meant that spring was finally on its way. These were the first of the birds she'd seen for the season. She'd been so excited to watch them, having heard their birdsong from her window, that she'd raced out into the chilly morning air in her nightgown. Her Tante had found her moments later but remained watching from the ground.

Then, the song returned, sung by a voice which had yet been hardened with age and sorrow. So did the tears.

"Why do you cry, Tante?" the younger her had called down. *"Do the birds make you sad?"*

"No, my little kestrel," her Tante had replied. *"They are friends I have not seen for time."*

"Then you should be happy, no?"

"I am," she'd replied with a heavy sniffle. *"I am…"*

The memory faded.

Her Tante had stopped speaking, lost to her own memories. Loneliness sprouted between the wooden floorboards. Silence sat beside them in the bathhouse.

The lyrics which had lived for many years in her head, her heart, and which she'd long associated with her Tante's fascination with birds, suddenly gained a darker significance.

"Tante… is this only a story?" she asked.

A heavy sigh escaped her Tante's lips, a love letter to the silence and sorrows. "Time turns all memories into stories. But the scars remain. Burn marks in a heart no ointment can heal."

"What happened to them?"

"Like the birds, they were too different to ever come together. The fire of their love was too strong to contain. It ripped through the lands, reminding everyone why the two worlds could never collide."

So, it is hopeless… Keziah thought. Warm tears rolled down her cheeks, dripping into the bath to get lost in the waters. They disappeared, unsanctimonious, as though they were not the product of prayer and passion, but simple droplets of common salt water.

Keziah wiped them from her cheeks and mumbled, "I guess she and I are both cursed by Iturri, then…"

"Oh?" Her Tante paused her combing. "How so?"

"We fell in love with men we could never have, by no fault of our own," Keziah replied, sinking deeper into the bathwater. "And all I wanted was to practice my powers… To see beyond the forest…" The words, though true, tasted sour on her tongue. There was much more to it, and she'd known it from the very beginning. "Iturri is a sinful god. Toying with hearts this way. I never asked to fall in love…"

Her Tante chuckled softly as she began to lather Keziah's hair with the ginger lily sap. She massaged it into her scalp, a sensation that used to bring comfort, but in her current state, Keziah felt nothing but pain.

"Iturri is a maker of chaos to be sure," her Tante added. "But I'd wager it is not looking to break your heart, rather test your resolve."

"What do you mean?"

"What allure held the rest of the world? Why did you feel the need to leave?"

"Because…" Frustration riddled her voice. It came from a place deep within that Keziah had scarcely allowed herself to acknowledge. It came from monotonous days and lonely nights wishing that she were free to live the life she chose, rather than the one her father had decided. "I wanted to be seen, be heard..."

Be loved, for just being me...

"Well, it sounds like Iturri gave you exactly that. This boy of yours, he saw you, no?" Keziah nodded. "He heard you?" her Tante continued. Again, she nodded in silence. "Iturri gave you a taste of what you wanted. Now, it has decided to push you, to see how badly you want it, how far you are willing to go to be that which you claim to be—"

"So this is all a game?" Keziah hissed, a fresh batch of angry tears rolling down her cheeks. "Like a stupid game of Go, where it gets to watch on as we lose every piece on our playing board, helplessly trying to move forward, and then laugh at us when there is nothing left..."

"Oh, my little kestrel, don't you see? Love is not a thing to be won or lost. Love—real love—is something enduring, all-encompassing. It underpins the very fabric of every emotion. And it doesn't leave. It lingers, present in your every breath, and rippling outwards with your every heartbeat. So, no. Iturri has not done this to watch you suffer, nor does it play games. Rather, if you ask it for a blessing, it tests your worthiness."

It still sounds like I am being toyed with...

Keziah never meant to feel this way. If it weren't for Caspar's arrow, she would've gone about her life like always. She'd have been as immovable as her father—and probably twice as bitter. She resented the way Caspar, in a matter of days, had broken her, turned her into a completely different person. But more importantly, she resented the fact that she could not be with him.

"It hurts, Tante. Too much," she sobbed into her knees,

a trail of shivers carving their way over her shoulders and down her spine.

Her Tante rinsed the ginger sap from her hair and the tears from her face. "Then, you can be sure it is love."

"If this is love, I don't want it. I don't want to feel this way…"

"But you must. May we all be lucky to experience the sting of love at least once in this lifetime. For, without it, we are nothing more than plants without sunlight… However, if you still feel you need to air out your grievances, I'd suggest a visit to the chapel. A long, hard conversation may be in order. What better place than a chapel to be heard by a god? Or, if you care not for talking, then to at least count your blessings?"

"But Tante, there's nothing I can do. You saw the smoke. They wish to kill him."

"Hmm…" Her Tante let out a heavy sigh. "If that is what you truly feel, then you have only two options…" She rose from the floor beside the bath and deposited the comb on one of the shelves, making a show of wiping her hands clean. "Either you sit there and sulk in your dirty bathwater until your skin shrivels like a berry in the sun, or you do something about it."

Keziah raised her head and turned to face her. "But Tante—"

"Regardless, you will never insult the game of Go in front of me again," she scoffed. "I don't know who you are, but I know you are not my Keziah." The sharpness of her tone startled her. Keziah's breath hitched at the sight of her Tante's cold eyes. Their usual warmth had been smothered, almost past the point of recognition. "My Keziah would not hide her tears in bathwater." The screen door closed behind her, leaving Keziah alone with the sting of her words.

Her eyes lingered in the space her Tante had just left. The bathwater had long since gone cold though the hot stones sat only a small stretch away. Goosebumps crawled down her arms, though she couldn't bring herself to move.

What had her Tante meant? She couldn't possibly expect Keziah to stand up to her father again, right? Especially not after dragging her away from his fury-driven hand…

Keziah reached a hand to her cheek, remembering the strike. It had come as more of a shock than anything. He'd never hit her before, certainly not in a way that was so…personal. She'd never imagined him as capable of such a thing. But then, she'd never imagined herself befriending—let alone falling in love with—an *Argia*.

The light overhead faded. Keziah cast her gaze upwards to the opening in the thatched roof. A waft of the dark cloud blotted out the remnants of light that made it through the canopy, calling her back to the urgency of the situation. Keziah's blood ran colder than the bathwater.

Time was running out.

She was the only hope Caspar had, and here she sat, wallowing in a pool of her own tears whilst leaving him to his fate.

The memory of Caspar—his warmth, his laughter, his kindness—burned as hot as the desert sun in her heart. No matter how hard, no matter how impossible it seemed, she could not abandon him. Her Tante's words finally made sense.

How could she call it love if she didn't fight for it?

If there was any hope in saving him, she'd have to act now. She might never change her father's mind, but she could at least change the outcome. Besides, her Tante was right. She had never been one to take no for an answer.

Keziah scrambled from the tub. She hardly dried her skin before slipping into the nightgown and bolting for the door. The scent of lavender oil lingered on her skin, trailing behind her as she ran. Her wet feet padded lightly this time on the wooden floor, careful not to slip in her haste. Her heart pounded in her chest. She couldn't let anyone catch her—she wouldn't.

No one would ever stand between her and Caspar again.

❦ CHAPTER 17 ❦

WITH THE VILLAGE BUSTLING AT THE announcement of the trial, Keziah knew better than to follow the well-trodden wooden walkways towards the chapel. Instead, she slipped back into secretive old habits, climbing down from the balcony and traversing the forest floor barefoot, away from prying eyes.

Whether she'd intended to or not, her Tante had already revealed more than enough about where they were keeping Caspar. Though, considering how dense her brothers were, it was no stretch of the imagination to see why they would've chosen the one entirely rock-based building in the village.

Keziah's feet made little sound as she raced across the damp woodland floors. Each step was a cold embrace of the earth. The dirt, still moist with the morning's dew, attempted to slow her stride—a far cry from the compact soils of Caspar's lands. Yet, with each confident stride, she found her strength growing. As if the lands themselves were crying out for her to use them, to remember her legacy. The grounds hummed as though reminding her that she had not been blessed for nothing—that her powers had been waiting for something like this.

For purpose.

The temple lay deep in the forest, in the centre of a clearing no man could maintain. It was as though nature itself would not allow weeds to grow on hallowed grounds. Beams of light danced over the temple roof, shifting with the rustling leaves overhead. A babbling brook rimmed the clearing—the only other sound for miles that hadn't been muffled by the dark foliage. That, and the air leaving her chest in heavy puffs.

It was not dressed in the same fine wooden carvings or gold embellishments as the rest of the village. Still, it was one of the few buildings in the village made entirely of the stone, as if to say *Iturri*, their all-powerful deity, could not live in the same structures as the common folk. It needed a palace, even if only the concept of one. Aside from the sparkling flecks in the granite alone, the temple was plain, bare. Lacklustre in every way. Not even the large wooden doors gave any indication of the value of this building. Yet, no passersby would escape the immediate shift in the air upon approach. The poignant cold that befell all, regardless of season. No ears were free of the introspective hum of hearts that transcended lifetimes. It was as if the forest itself were chanting songs of the spirit, though no tunes filled the air. No golden plaque or finery was needed to command respect. This building spoke the language of soil and soul. This clearing demanded reverence.

Keziah gulped, biting down on her nerves as she tiptoed around to the back side of the building. A simple trellis with roses at the point of blooming lined the back wall. Above it lay an open window. She breathed a sigh of relief. She'd found her way in.

Each step closer to the temple made her palms vibrate. They sang with power she'd scarcely felt before, despite having frequented the temple multiple times in her life. Her heart raced. In spite of it all, the only thing she could think about was Caspar.

The window towered high above her mockingly. Keziah pursed her lips. It would be sacrilege to ruffle the ground, and she couldn't raise herself up to the window without causing a ruckus. The only silent way through would be through the thorns.

Without a second thought, Keziah reached into the bushes and began climbing the branches, fighting against the thorns. They burrowed themselves into her palms, ripped at her bare skin, but still she climbed. She winced in silence, holding back each urge to scream out in pain. Tears welled at the edges of her eyes, blurring her vision, but she wouldn't stop. She couldn't.

Keziah was almost at the top when one of the traitorous branches gave out beneath her weight.

"Ahh!" she cried as she slipped a good way down before finally catching hold of a sturdy branch. Her yelp broke through the mystical silence. It echoed around her like the whistles of mockingbirds, making fun of her misfortune. Blood and tears dripped from her in equal measure. "All this for a stupid hunter…" Keziah muttered, blinking back tears. She wanted to wring his neck for putting them in this mess, but above all, she needed him safe.

Someone surely heard her scream. Keziah knew she had to act fast. If her brothers or her father were alerted, the wounds would be the least of her worries.

Undeterred and prodded on by a wickedly self-righteous sense of love, Keziah regained her footing and began the climb anew. As she inched higher and higher, she noticed the roses beginning to blossom before her, as if sapping her life force with each prick, each drop of spilled blood.

By the time Keziah hoisted herself onto the windowsill, the silk nightgown was torn and stained a dark red. She wiped away the beads of sweat on her upper lip, the scent of iron filling her nostrils. Her breathing was jagged and sharp, and still, it only scarcely filled the silence of the clearing.

Inside, the room was dark. No sacred candles or even the dying embers of old incense to be found. The only light came from the singular window, which her form now blocked. The faintest smell of ash lingered in the stagnant air. If she hadn't known better, she would've thought the room entirely vacant.

Keziah dropped down as gracefully as possible given her injuries, barely landing on her feet as she hit the hard granite floors. In the centre of the room, she spied a mass of beautiful auburn curls and the boy they belonged to. His hands and feet were bound, his mouth gagged, his eyes blindfolded. His head hung low over his chest.

Tears filled her eyes as she beheld him. She could hardly tell from so far away if he was breathing, but she prayed to all the stars she'd seen in the desert sky that he was alive.

"Caspar...?" she whispered, unsure if the words had left her lips at all. She could hardly hear her own voice over the sound of her beating heart.

To her surprise, Caspar's ears perked up. He moved his head around to find the source of the noise. Relief trickled into her heart, but she scarcely allowed herself to latch onto it. Not before she was certain he was alright.

Keziah tiptoed towards him, traversing the cold granite tiles with caution. Part of her felt that any sudden movement might cause him to disappear. As she approached, the scent of ash and blood increased, mingling with that of her own. It took all her strength not to break down out of the sheer, unrelenting pain of her own wounds. It seemed Caspar was no better off.

Their bodies, reflections of the damage of outdated traditions and prejudices. Each gash on her skin was a mirror of his bruises. Her stomach recoiled thinking about it.

Keziah raised a trembling hand to his bruised cheek. Her fingers grazed his skin; her touch, delicate and fleeting, in fear that she would do more damage.

His skin was cold, clammy. It reminded her of the unfriendly grip of the sea from her encounter with death. The eerie blue light of the morning did nothing to dampen her worries. Rather, it highlighted the injuries peeking out from beneath his blindfold, turning them a deep shade of purple.

Despite her hesitation, Caspar leaned into her palm. Beneath her touch, his skin began to warm. His body drew close, like a moth to flame. And just like that, relief began its slow settlement—laying down roots in her heart, fighting the hesitation in her soul. Then, she slid her hand down his cheek, seeking out the knots of his gag and blindfold. Her fingers trembled as they worked through the bindings, still fearful one wrong move might cause additional pain.

Oh, Caspar. What have they done to you?

"Keziah..." he breathed once she'd released his gag, as

though he too were afraid she'd vanish. The sound of her name on his bruised lips sent shivers down her spine. And then, when the blindfold dropped, he gazed upon her in splintered reverie—not as his saviour, but as a spectre, uniquely his in torture. Dark circles rimmed his glistening bloodshot eyes. The gold of his irises fought the grim blue of the morning light. As they focused on her, they widened, their fires reignited. He withheld tears, transfixed by her presence as though he gazed upon a ghost—as though he'd believed he would never see her again. "Are you...real?"

"I am," Keziah replied, running her fingers through his hair slowly, allowing him to settle in the understanding that she was present, safe. That they were here, together.

Caspar leaned into her hand further; his breath echoed in the silence. It came in heavy pants at first, but as he softened into her, so did his breathing. Between two fading sighs, Keziah caught the faint sound of the words *thank you*.

With her own breathing jagged from the climb and the nerves, Keziah fixed her focus on the feel of his weak heartbeat rippling through the floors to distract herself from her own pain. It came in slowly, softly. Almost ephemeral. Yet, she clung to it the way she'd clung to him after drowning. Back then, it had been her tether back to the world of the living. Now, even in all its faintness, she realized it was the anchor to the world of her dreams.

And it was fading.

Keziah fixed all her attention on it, as though her own life depended on it. She'd never noticed the way it matched up perfectly with hers. Perhaps she hadn't wanted to, not until now. Though they'd been brought up miles away, they somehow shared the beat of the same drum. Slowly but surely, it started to regain some of its strength. As though her presence had brought it back to life.

Soon, its beat grew stronger, wilder, uninhibited in his chest. Hers kept in tune, almost as though they'd been calling out for each other—even in separation. It reminded Keziah of a lullaby, the low thrum of a familiar song, and one she'd known long before they'd ever met. It was as though their hearts had known—had always known—what or who they were looking for.

A home, a haven, a happily ever after...

"I was so worried..." she added. "I don't understand it... Why are we here? The last thing I remember was..."

Flashes of the water appeared again, aided on by the shifting morning light. The memory alone of the saltwater stinging her nose and eyes and threatened to free her tears. She heard him calling her name in the distance, as if they were once again separated by waves. He called again and again, until finally, she snapped out of it.

"I had to keep you safe," he admitted softly. He retreated from her hand, guilt marring his face as though the confession were of sin. "And there... I couldn't."

"Are you insane?!" Keziah clenched her fists at her sides, digging her nails into her palms to quell her annoyance. His confession had triggered her pride, the part of her that loathed any show of weakness in herself. He'd practically admitted he didn't think her capable of fending for herself—just like her father. "How dare you do something so...so...reckless?!"

A tremor rumbled to life in the grounds beneath them, punctuating her frustration. Keziah could hardly sense anything over the rage building inside her.

"Keziah, you almost died," he replied, straining against the pain in his throat. "I wasn't going to let that happen again."

"And what about you?! Between those boys at the beach…the guards of the forest…" she continued. With each one she listed off, the tremor grew.

Caspar turned from her, casting a furtive glance upwards.

"Keziah—"

"I never asked you to help. I never asked you to save me…" The words felt heavy, laden with a guilt she'd scarcely voiced, yet she couldn't stop herself. Something inside her pushed them out before she could process what she was saying. It made her sick, the weakness behind the admission. The girl she was before him would never have felt something like this. The knowing that there had been nothing she could've done to stop him, let alone save him, ate away at her spirit. "I never asked you to make me feel like this…"

The rafters groaned overhead.

"Keziah, breathe!" Caspar cried out.

Keziah froze, only now noticing the patter of the falling debris around them. The shaking continued for a second more before settling, allowing the tail end of his words to echo in the hollow hall. Keziah stared up at the rafters, her heartbeat ringing out loudly in her ears. The sensation had come on too suddenly only to vanish even more so for it to have been an earthquake. When she looked back at Caspar, specifically at the caution lining his brow, she realized it had been no thing of nature at all.

Was that…me?

The thought sent her reeling. Someone would have felt the tremor, heard the groaning rafters. Someone would come. And if they caught her in here with him, there would be no hope for saving him.

"You're bleeding…" Caspar said, breaking her stream of worries.

Keziah furrowed her brow as she closed her eyes, unable to look at him without breaking down. He was battered and bruised, being held captive by foreign powers, practically on death's doorstep, and still, he was concerned for her. Hot streams of flustered tears rolled down her cheeks, and this time, she hadn't the strength to stop them.

"Stop it!" she yelled, unable to contain the rage any longer. "Think of yourself for once."

"Please don't cry," he whispered.

"Why did you do it?" she hissed. She ignored his comment out of sheer frustration. "Why risk your life for me…?" Caspar had absolutely nothing to gain from saving her. In fact, just being in her vicinity had put him in arguably more danger than hunting ever would. Still, he insisted on being there for her. He was even willing to give up his own life to see her safely home.

Keziah hated how much her heart yearned for such a connection, for a person like him. But her mind fought back with the cruellest of thoughts. For, what had she ever done to deserve such treatment?

"The truth?" Caspar asked, his voice delicate.

She nodded, but no answer came. After another minute of silence, she heard his voice again.

"Keziah?"

"What?!" she growled, her entire body vibrating with nervous energy.

"Look at me… Please."

Her throat burned from holding back her emotions. Keziah took a deep breath and forced herself to meet his gaze, unable to remove the film of tears lining her eyes.

In the dim light of the chapel, the blue of the shadowy stone walls crept over his skin, but somehow, not even that could extinguish his fire. He looked at her the same way he had that first night they spent together. It was a look that Keziah's hesitant heart had already memorized, in case she would never see it again.

Even before the words left his lips, her breath hitched in her throat.

"I could no longer imagine my life without you."

His words, so plainly spoken, pierced her deeper than any arrow ever could.

They filled a hole in her chest that she scarcely acknowledged existed. And that was when the realization finally hit. Her Tante was right, she had changed. She was not the same girl who made shallow demands of others while wishing for a life beyond the confines of their village. She'd unintentionally gotten her wish and, in the process, found an adventure grander than any she'd ever imagined.

She could no longer deny it. The Keziah she'd known—the Keziah she'd been—had died that day when the arrow pierced her skin. The Keziah she was now was overrun with fear, the greatest of all being the worry that their time together was over before it ever truly got started.

What if she couldn't save him? What if she lost her only chance at happiness? What if it was all for nothing?

An eerie silence settled between them in the absence of words and tremors. It felt too quiet, too calm considering the gravity of the moment. In her mind, the world was on the verge of collapse, but the sturdy granite walls around them remained as rigid and upright as ever. No breeze filtered in from up on high. No shadows danced between them. No loud roars of thunder or terrifying earthquakes in sight. Only the lingering memory of the words voiced aloud, yet they were enough to send her spiralling.

When she didn't respond, he added, "I never meant to return you to this place to be caged. I never meant to hurt you."

"Oh, Caspar, you are ridiculous…" she whispered as she dropped to the floor beside him. She threw her arms around his neck and held him tight. He in turn nestled his chin into the crook of her neck. He smelled of dirt and ash—of home.

She'd confessed as much to her Tante. This boy with pauper's clothes and auburn curls had taken the heart she'd given freely. And she now knew her affections were not one-sided.

"It's okay—we're okay…" he whispered into her skin.

"No, not yet. Caspar, we need to get you out of here," she began, sweeping the tears away as she looked for a way to break Caspar's binds. "I will not let you suffer anymore."

Keziah pressed a hand to the ground and visualized the stone beneath it turning into a stake. As she retracted her hand, the vision in her mind became reality. The stone pulled away from the surrounding floor in the shape of something that would help pry off the bonds.

"Don't move," she told him as she made her way around with the stake. She stuck it between the fibres and wiggled it, hoping to cut through the tight ropes.

She was almost there.

Her spirits lifted when the first snap of the ropes came through. She could almost taste their freedom.

But then, the doors to the chamber flew open.

❧CHAPTER 18❧

SHE'D APPEARED OUT OF NOWHERE LIKE an angel—a phoenix.

Keziah.

The sombre light filtering in from the high windows of the chamber wrapped her in an ethereal glow. As the bandage fell from his eyes, relief flooded through him. She was safe, she was unharmed. She was here, with him. Part of him thought it was only a dream, a hallucination of the mind close to death. The righteous part of him wished it was, for he knew how much trouble she would be in otherwise. But with each waft of lavender that bled from her damp hair, he knew she was here, she was real. And she was bleeding.

"Keziah…"

Caspar had spent the entire night locked in the room, bound and gagged for having dared trespass onto *Harri* lands. It didn't seem to matter that he'd returned the chief's daughter. He was a villain in their eyes and always would be.

Only an elderly woman had taken the slightest bit of pity on him. He'd noticed her clinging to the shadows upon his arrival, never properly catching a glimpse of her face, but knowing by the cross of her arms and the solemn frown she'd worn that she had been opposed to his capture. His suspicions were confirmed at around midnight when, at a point before finally relenting to a painful sleep, he heard the soft patter of footsteps. They drew near, moving swiftly across the floor, unlike his captors' stampede-inspired clomping.

She'd come in silently, trailed by the soft scent of lavender and incense. Again, he'd thought it was his mind playing tricks on him. Only when he felt the soft touch of her hands removing the gag had he realized he was not alone.

"You saved her," the woman had said.

Caspar tentatively nodded, unsure whom he was addressing. The men who had bound him had been brutal. They were as thick as tree trunks and sturdy, as though they had been made of stone. This woman was softer in her approach. Kind, in an almost motherly way. The way she'd released the knot on the gag spoke of tenderness and patience—things he scarcely remembered since his mother had died.

The woman did not remove the blindfold, however.

"Why?" she had asked, to which Caspar replied,

"Because I've never seen a fire brighter than the one in her eyes."

When no reply came, Caspar wondered once more if it had all been a dream. Until suddenly, without another word, he felt the gentle nudge of something sweet against his lips. He opened his mouth and took a bite. It tasted of oat and honey, with a hint of cinnamon. The woman fed him two more before he heard her rise.

"Hold on to that faith, young Argia. Your battle is not yet lost," she whispered. The echo of her swift feet lingered only a second longer than her words.

Somewhere between then and now, he'd drifted off to sleep, imagining Keziah in his arms, unincumbered and in love. Perhaps, had they been different people, such a thing might have been possible. Simple, even.

Until now, he'd scarcely expected to see her again. Thankfully, Iturri had once again decided to prove him wrong.

"Why are you here?" Her gentle voice pleaded with him for a reason he knew would only hurt her. Before this, he'd believed he was doing the right thing, that she would've left at some point. But the fear and anger behind her plea told him he was wrong. His blood ran cold.

She hadn't wanted to leave.

The nervous energy rippling from her as she paced about the floor brought back the memory of their time on the roof. She'd confessed to him in earnest her hatred of her father's treatment towards her, how he'd practically caged her and enforced his will upon her without considering her wishes.

He'd done the same. She'd trusted him with this knowledge, with her boundaries, and he'd accidentally broken that trust. He hadn't meant to, but he'd done *exactly* what her father had.

And because of it, death aside, he might lose her forever.

Panic settled over him, the same panic that had driven him to bring her here, but this time, he would not let it get the better of him.

"I'm sorry," he said, meeting her gaze of cold fury with

a plea of his own. "I know sorry is not enough for this… I never meant to hurt you."

She raised an arm in what he thought was meant to be a strike. The next thing he knew, her arms were around him in an embrace that he wished would never end. Caspar nuzzled his face into the hollow of her neck, fighting back tears of relief, though he felt her own dripping down his back.

"It's okay…" he whispered, planting a kiss into her neck. "We're okay…" His heart sank hearing her sobs. He wished more than anything to be freed of his restraints, to be able to embrace her properly as he had on the shores of the beach. To hold her until she had no tears left to cry. "Don't cry for me," he added. "An angel like you should never cry for anything but happiness in this lifetime…"

Sadly, their reunion was cut short.

The same two burly men that had dragged him in the room last night burst through the doors. Beyond the precipice of the chapel walls, a fire crackled in the distance. Its smoke a heavy black cloud drifting in the morning air. Their shadows stretched across the floor like the hands of death reaching out for him. Red halos of firelight rimmed their bodies. They were the image of hatred and malice.

"Out of the way, Keziah," the first one said.

"You shouldn't be here," added the second.

Despite their words, Keziah did not retreat. Instead, she wiped the tears from her eyes and turned to face the men. The energy around her quickly shifted. She puffed out her chest, hiding the pain and sorrow they'd shared in favour of defiance. Her body acted like a barricade, protecting Caspar from the men. Little as she was, she would not back down. She refused to move.

"Keziah, don't do this…" Caspar whispered to her. "It's not worth it… I'm not—"

"I will not let you harm him," she growled, ignoring his plea. The ferocity in her voice harked back to that first moment they'd met in the forest. The version of her that surfaced was that of a wounded animal—one with an unpredictable temper. Caspar held his breath, unsure of what to expect from either side. He figured if those men knew what was good for them, they would back down.

But the men were not moved by her outburst. They drew closer, their bare feet falling heavy on the ground like the sound of an executioner's drum.

"Keziah—"

"Step out of the way, sister, or we will move you ourselves," said the first man, the elder of the two.

The sunlight faded behind him, hidden behind the black smoke and morning fog.

Caspar looked upon the faces of his captors, noticing finally the threads of their familial tapestry. They maintained Keziah's dark hair and vibrant eyes, but the similarities forked there. The men had different tones of Keziah's chestnut skin and variations in their noses and jaws. The two of them shared more in common between themselves than with her, but time, it seemed, had hardened them in ways her younger age would not yet permit.

"Ishan, Karthic, I am warning you," she hissed, unmoved by their threats.

A low tremor stirred from within the chapel's stone walls. It was barely noticeable given the tensions hanging in the air, except to those who were paying attention. Had Caspar not experienced a similar tremor only moments before, he might have missed it. He might have thought the reason lay beyond the chapel walls. But he knew better—he knew the truth.

It had come from her. Given the power she wielded, the earth responded, like a willing lapdog, to her rising anger. Given the potential for destruction that she harboured within, his eyes fell to her hands, knowing before they arrived that he would find them trembling.

But, unlike before, this would not end in silence. If this continued, it would be a war.

"Have you not done enough to sully our name, sister?" said the second, taking another intrusive step towards them.

The tremors grew.

The shaking loosened dust and pebbles from the rafters. They rained down from the ceiling in warning, following the path of cracks that had started to form in the granite.

"Keziah," Caspar tried in a gentle voice, hoping to stop the quake before it began, knowing that the resulting destruction would leave them no room for escape. "Please stop…"

But again, she chose not to hear him. "Come any closer and it will be the last step you take."

Her words carried weight, heavier than the shaking walls. Her eldest brother's eyes darted to the shaking doorframe and the growing debris. "Karthic, stand down."

The younger of the two flared his nostrils towards them. "Ishan," he replied to his brother, never once taking his eyes from Caspar and Keziah, "you cannot allow her to continue with this nonsense."

"This *nonsense*, Karthic, is my life," Keziah barked. "And I will fight for my freedom to live and love until my dying breath."

Caspar's heart skipped a beat at the sound of that word.

Love. It felt like vindication. His feelings were not one-sided. "Keziah…" he whispered, his voice hesitant.

Cracks climbed the granite walls. Only he and Ishan seemed to notice. The other two were locked in an intense stare down, neither one willing to relinquish the control their egos exerted.

Ishan took a single retreating step. He, like Caspar, watched the unsteady foundations in fear that the whole chapel would come crashing down around them. His brow furrowed in frustration as he searched for the source of the tremors. When his questioning gaze landed on Keziah's clenched fists, his eyes widened. Fear carved lines through his forehead.

Keziah and Karthic, however, continued their brawl in spite of the trembling.

"You have grown arrogant in your absence, sister," growled Karthic as he took up a fighting stance.

"And you, somehow more ignorant," she replied, moving to match him.

"Keziah, please. It's not worth it…" Caspar pleaded, feeling his heart begin to race.

Ishan gripped his brother's shoulder and tugged. "Brother, the walls."

For the first time since he'd entered, Karthic glanced around the room. The trembling continued, the sound beginning to echo.

"Keziah, stop this!" yelled Ishan, but his hesitant demand was met with the sound of a loud crack above their heads.

The altar behind Caspar shook violently before tumbling to the floor. He curled into a tighter ball, trying to avoid the debris. The crash sent a plume of dust into the air.

"Enough!" called a voice whose timbre seemed to break spirits.

* * *

The sound of her father's voice boomed loud over the cracking granite. Keziah held her breath as he moved through the plume of dust, parting it like the wind through the willow trees. His green eyes glowed in the blue of the chapel light.

"Enough with this nonsense," he repeated. His voice was low and damaged like the growl of a lone wolf.

Keziah felt the sharp knives of fear and inadequacy digging into her heart at the mere sound of it. The handprint across her face had not yet faded into the vaults of traumas past. She'd already tried and failed to stand up to him once. Retreating a step, she made sure Caspar's body was protected from any unexpected outbursts. Her father had already proven he had no problems with violence towards his family. She doubted love would be lost on a stranger— an *Argia* at that.

"I will not have you wrecking this chapel over a creature like that," he added, disdain weaving itself through his words. He took a step towards her, but this time, she didn't falter.

With each insult-ridden reference to Caspar, her ire grew. It emboldened her in ways nothing had before. At the risk of another strike, she countered. "Father, you will not speak about Caspar like that. Nor will I allow you to harm him in any way."

He glowered at her. "You, allowing me?" he mocked. "What power do you have over a chief? Stand down before you get hurt."

"I refuse," Keziah hissed. The chapel began to shake

once more, but this time it was intentional. She took a deep breath, centring herself as she focused on the ground beneath her father's feet. With the next flick of her wrist, the ground clamped shut over his feet. Surprise came over his face, but before he could react, Keziah stomped her foot to the ground, lifting the fallen pebbles into the air. They hovered around her body like a swarm of hornets.

"It appears you have disobeyed me in more ways than one, daughter," her father growled as he cracked his knuckles. He glanced past her at Caspar, and then at the stones. His expression was calculating, cold, and entirely unfamiliar. Then, one after the other, his large feet easily broke free of their stone prisons, the sound echoing throughout the chapel. "You were told not to use those powers." He swatted at the air with a single hand, pulling the stones from her control and casting them to the floor. "You were told never to stray too far from this village." Even her brothers retreated as he stepped towards her. "And now, you forsake your own people over a child of our enemies…"

"He is no more an enemy to us than I," Keziah replied, her voice faltering slightly at the raw display of his power.

Irritation rippled from him, rumbling the way the mountain does before a rockslide. "Your insistence is becoming impertinence, and I will not have a child of mine disgrace our people in such a way." Her father raised his voice. "Step away from that boy, or I will move you myself."

When Keziah refused, her father swung his bear-sized palm to the left, sending the floor shifting like a wave beneath her feet to throw her off her balance. Before it could hit, she stomped another foot to the ground; the vibrations of her blow crashed into the wave, stopping it in its tracks. To her father's chagrin, she was not backing down.

"I've already told you, Father. I will not let you harm him."

"Father, be merciful," pleaded Ishan from behind. "She doesn't know what she is doing."

But their father ignored him. "I fear I have been too lenient with you, child. You were given too much freedom after your mother died, but this ends now."

Though her heart was full of fear, Keziah squared up against her father. He fired off a warning shot—a large stone from the broken altar hurled in her direction. Keziah lifted a part of the ground like a shield, protecting her and Caspar from the attack.

Her father grew impatient. He fired off another set of stones towards her from all angles. Keziah defended them still, raising and releasing various pillars of stone to block. The strikes came at her faster and more furiously.

"You think there is justice in protecting this one boy from his grave?" her father boomed over the echoes of his attacks. "Have you forgotten our history? His people sent hundreds of ours to their deaths; burned them alive. And you stand there protecting him?"

"I have not forgotten anything, Father," Keziah replied between heavy breaths. Even in his old age, her father's stamina was impressive. Greater than hers by far. Aside from her spat with Karthic only moments before, Keziah had never used her powers in an actual fight. This was a true test of her strength, and she feared he could feel her courage wavering. "But Caspar is not like the rest of his people..."

Her father's scowl deepened. "Pears do not fall from peach trees. The wound on your arm is a testament to his nature."

Keziah knew her father was restraining himself. He did not truly want to hurt her, but he knew as well as she did that there would be no backing down in their war of egos. The intensity of his strikes grew. Her legs began to shake, absorbing shockwave after shockwave. Sweat trickled from her brow. But she couldn't give up.

"It was a mistake! And rather than leaving me there to die, he carried me alone, back to his village, and tended to me as good as any healer." Her heart raced, trying to keep up with her movements. Her lungs burned with the urgency of her breathing. "He saved me from death not once, but twice. And on top of that, he brought me here to you. He is no threat. If anything, you should be thanking him—"

"Thanking him?! His head should be at the other end of my spear for having stolen you away in the first place."

"Do you even hear me when I talk?!" Keziah roared. The temple trembled violently, sending her father staggering backwards. Another shower of dust and pebbles fell from the ceiling. Keziah used the break to her advantage. She placed her feet firmly on the ground and regained her fighting stance. "He is the *only* reason I am alive today. Another in his place might have left me for dead, if only for the fact that I am *Harri* and he is *Argia*. Yet, here I stand, alive and well, *because of* him." As she spoke, she swept her foot across the floor, launching the debris from his attacks back towards her father. He blocked most but not all, having been caught off guard by the quake. "You speak of justice," she called. "Yet, where is your sense of the word?" She wiped the sweat from her brow and fired off a larger stone. "You would kill an innocent over nothing more than your own prejudice—"

"You have no idea what you are talking about!" He regained his footing, swatting aside the rest of her attack as if it were nothing more than leaves in the breeze. The burning fury in his green eyes shining through the dust. "You admit yourself they tried to kill you on the basis of your race. Where then do you find *justice?*"

"I was there, Father. I have seen it—their fear, their hatred…"

Keziah was reminded of Caspar's father, of how he'd first treated her. He had been harsh, but she realized quickly that he had been hurting. A hurt that knows no bounds. A cruelty that any of her tribe might have shown to an *Argia*. She hadn't realized it before, but she found this same wounded cruelty staring back at her now, reflected in her father's eyes.

"Their prejudice… Yet, in the face of such prejudice, there are still those, like Caspar, who see past the tortured shadows of the past. Those who show kindness and humility, in spite of difference." Keziah straightened, afraid no longer of the repercussions of her actions. "Prejudice is a learned thing, Father, and one that knows no tribe or race…" Tears streamed down her cheeks. "You have fostered the same prejudice in our town which you believe resides in theirs. But I am tired of falling for the same rhetoric. I want to be an example of what could be, rather than another reason things cannot change."

Her father's brows furrowed, his jaw tightening, but he said nothing.

"You say you hate them for their actions, but yours are no different. You are actively choosing to continue the cycle of hatred and fear. You are the wolf chasing its tail, and whose bite bites him back."

Her father's eyes darkened. "Your words, daughter, are just that. Words," he said. "Do you believe they are enough to change centuries of enmity? Enough to heal wounds that have festered for generations?"

"Bitterness begets bitterness, Father. Words alone are not enough—will never be enough. But they are a start. And if we don't start somewhere, then what hope is there for any of us? Are we destined to keep this cycle of destruction going forever? To teach our children the same hatred we were taught?"

"It is not so simple, Keziah. You think I don't want peace? I've dreamed of it. But dreams don't keep our people safe. Tradition does."

"The same tradition that would have talents wasted based on sex?"

"I will not lose you like I lost her!" yelled her father. His voice shook the temple walls. A loud crack followed. They all turned to face the ceiling. The next thing any of them knew, part of the structure had caved in.

Keziah froze, fear riddling her body. A ringing sound filled her ears, drowning out the screams of her father and brothers. All she could do was watch as the ceiling came crashing down upon her.

CHAPTER 19

THE WORLD AROUND HER WAS ENGULFED IN white. The crash had left her ears ringing, but soon that died too. For a moment, everything felt still. Quiet. Other than the peace that flooded through her body, Keziah felt nothing. For a moment, she questioned whether she was still alive.

Then, the cold crept in.

The ringing was replaced with birds chirping in the distance. The white dust drifted overhead, giving way to the dark canopy. Lights twinkled above her, poking through the smoke and foliage. Exposed streams of sunlight glittered in her eyes like stars in the desert night sky. The morning air poured in through the hole in the ceiling, breathing new life into the ancient tomb.

Keziah took a deep breath in, savouring this strange new freedom. Staring up at the glittering canopy, she felt a weight lift from her chest.

Then, her father appeared through the sea of dust and

debris looking more like an apparition than a human. His tear-filled eyes glowed with humility. As though he'd witnessed a spirit rise from the shattered tomb. He said nothing. His face had blanched. His lips, though parted, made no sound. He merely watched on in silence. It all seemed so much like a dream that Keziah wondered if he truly was an apparition. She noticed his hands trembling at his sides.

Only then did she look down and notice the chained hands that wrapped around her torso. They were pale, bruised, and on the verge of bleeding. Another heartbeat raced behind her, one that had become so familiar to her over the past few days that she could've almost mistook it for her own. A heavy breath fell over her shoulder. The heat of it raised the hairs on her neck. The tangle of legs below did not belong to her alone.

Caspar, she realized. He'd saved her—*again*.

And this time, in front of everyone.

Slowly, he lifted his arms up over her head and released her. She turned to face him. Relief blossomed on his face as he gazed into her eyes. But Keziah couldn't hold his gaze, her eyes caught on the blood that trickled from the corner of his brow. Some of the debris had nicked him in the ordeal. Considering the weight of the old structure, they had been more than lucky in their escape.

Keziah placed a gentle hand on his cheek. "You're bleeding…"

"Are you okay?" Caspar asked, ignoring the comment entirely. His breath was laboured, having winded himself in the rescue.

"Never better," she replied, letting tears fill her eyes.

Caspar let a grin creep across his face as he beheld her.

He moved his bound hands to her forehead, sweeping away a lock of hair before pulling her in close. He rested his cold, trembling lips on her hairline, allowing his breath to slow, before planting a proper kiss.

Keziah pulled him in close, resting her ear on his chest. His heart was still racing. She wished to stay there in the aftermath of the disaster. To linger in the silence, pressed against him, memorizing the beat of his heart.

In front of them, the rest of the chapel roof lay in shambles. The streams of sunlight fell upon stones that had not seen light since their original mining over a century ago. The echo of feet shuffling through the rubble bounced around the walls. Her brothers crept out of the shadows and stood beside their father.

"Boys..." her father whispered finally, drawing her attention away from her saviour and towards her sombre brothers.

The next thing she knew, Ishan had her by the arm and pulled her to her feet.

"Let go of me!" she hissed.

Keziah was about to roar out in anger when Karthic appeared at her side. Instead of pulling her away as expected, he pulled out the key to Caspar's bindings. Keziah held her tongue as she watched her brother drop to the floor beside Caspar and unlock the chains. They dropped free with a loud clutter.

Caspar rubbed at the sore red spots on his wrists in silence. The dust from the old granite coated his hair and face, dulling his bright auburn hair. As he moved, it fell in soft showers from his curls, surrounding him in a white halo. When he looked over at her again, Keziah felt her heart flutter. His eyes twinkled like the lanterns dotting the forest. From wondering whether she'd ever see him again to having him standing before her, watching her with the eyes of the devout, Keziah felt relief flood her body.

In the stillness of the moment, Karthic reached out to him. Caspar looked down at the hand, considering the risk in taking it.

"Thank you…" Karthic mumbled. "For saving my little sister. You… We are in your debt."

Caspar took hold of Karthic's hand and nodded, sparing him the guilt of owning up to his earlier outbursts.

Outside, villagers had begun to gather. Their murmuring beyond the chapel walls mimicked the flapping of the birds that had fled the scene. They peered through the open doors, stepping on each other to catch a glimpse of the scene unfolding inside.

Keziah spied her Tante pushing frantically through the crowd. She raced over to Keziah, knocking Ishan out of the way as she smothered her in an embrace.

"My little kestrel! Are you okay?" She grabbed hold of Keziah's face, scanning it from all angles for signs of distress. "Oh, you poor child…" She prattled on about how worried she was, not allowing Keziah to get a word out. Then, in the only breath she took, her Tante jumped quickly to Caspar, pulling him into the same smothering embrace. "Thank you, thank you, thank you," she pleaded.

Startled, Caspar cast a glance over in her direction, to which Keziah responded with a light smirk. It took only a second before he relented to the hug—her Tante would never have let him out otherwise.

"Sister…" called the austere voice still lingering on the outskirts of the reunion. Only then did her Tante free Caspar from her doting clutches.

They all turned to face the chief, who stepped over the larger stones towards Caspar. He moved steadily, undeterred by his children or sister, stopping only when he was an arm's length away. His heavy heart echoed in the silence that fell over the chamber.

Keziah wanted to jump between them, to ensure Caspar's freedom and safety, but, to her surprise, her father simply cleared his throat.

"I may have been too harsh in my judgement of you. My daughter…" he said, casting a single glance over at Keziah. "She means the world to me. And, as she grows, I know I will no longer be able to protect her like I used to."

"Your daughter can protect herself," Caspar replied hesitantly.

"I know, but she is stubborn and quick to anger."

"Father, I—" Keziah interjected, but he continued over her, determined to get his words out before he changed his mind.

"So…" her father said, extending a hand to Caspar. It lingered in the air for a moment before he added, "I appreciate that she has found someone to look out for the dangers she cannot see."

Caspar accepted the hand, meeting her father's weighted gaze with the acknowledgement of his request and a promise.

Keziah watched in awe, unbridled tears spilling over her cheeks. She hadn't thought it possible, but her father had relented. Her father had never met an outsider to whom he'd even echoed the sentiment of respect. To Caspar, he gave more than an echo. He gave the full sentiment, willingly.

"And you," her father added as he turned to her. "You

are no longer my little kestrel. You have become a full-fledged falcon."

Unable to speak, Keziah wrapped her arms around her father's waist. Her tears stained his tunic. He embraced her fully; in a way she only remembered in the most distant of memories. "It seems this village has grown too small for you." He looked back at the crowd before addressing her again. "We are slow to change, though change itself is not impossible. I see that now. And yet…"

"This village is my home."

"And it always will be. But I fear you will feel stifled if you stay…"

Keziah squeezed her father tighter, realizing that finally she would be free to live life on her own terms. No one would tamper with her powers any longer.

* * *

Caspar rode back through the desert on horseback, the rhythmic beat of the hooves the only sound for miles. The glossy black coat of the mare beneath him shone almost copper under the rays of the sun. Keziah followed close behind on a matching white mare, her dark hair billowing behind her. The emerald fabric of her dress stood out against the muted reds and browns of the desert like a renegade forest leaf, like a speck of life in a wasteland. Heavy satchels hung from the horses' saddles, laden with supplies—gifts from Keziah's father and family. They returned like conquerors from battle, trailed by the clouds of dust kicked up by the horses.

Caspar couldn't remember the last time he'd seen so much food. Dates, nuts, tubers, fruits, ferns, and dried meats peeked through the folds of the satchels. Some things Caspar had heard of but never tried, others he had neither heard of nor could even imagine. Keziah's father had insisted that, if she was to stay with him, she would be well taken care of. It was a gesture of peace, of reluctant acceptance. The man might not have given his blessing with ease, but he had given it, nonetheless.

The lush greens of the forest swiftly fell away behind them, giving way to the rolling red sands of his homeland. The suddenness of such a change begged the question of whether the dense canopy had been nothing more than a fever dream. But then, she was still there beside him, a welcome reminder of the adventure that changed his life.

With Keziah by his side, not even the scorching heat of the desert sun seemed as bad. Seeing her there, a smile across her face as she galloped in the vastness of the desert, Caspar couldn't help but thank Iturri and all the stars above for having allowed him this one precious gift—this weed that had taken up root in his barren garden and brought it back to life. A weight lifted from his chest as he contemplated her, sharing in her freedom. She was no weed at all. She was a rose through and through—vibrant perfumed petals and a stem full of thorns.

And she was his.

The thought sent shivers down his spine. His body, though battered, vibrated with nervous energy. It was hard to believe that they were almost free.

Only one obstacle remained: his father.

Caspar had made the trek through the desert many times before, but something about this time felt different. Sure, he had Keziah bouncing along at his side, a more than welcome companion, but there was something more. The harsh desert sun did not burn as they used to. The shifting dusts seemed to lay dormant, aside from the trails being kicked up in their ride. Perhaps Iturri had shown favour, an easy passage for their suffering. But then, the physical symptoms appeared.

At first it was merely a sliver of cold sweat dripping down his brow. Then, a sudden cool rush across the back of his neck. Caspar had thought these were figments of his imagination, or else the early signs of desert fever, but when he cast his gaze to the skies, a pleasant sight greeted him.

Clouds.

And not just the wanton stragglers he was used to. No. These clouds stretched across the horizon, full and plentiful. They carried with them the sweet coolness of quenched lands.

He tugged at the reins, calling his horse to a halt. Keziah plodded on a pace or two before reining hers in and circling back to him.

"What's the matter?" she called, worry tracing the curve of her mouth. "Is everything okay?"

Caspar smiled. There was no way for him to explain the ephemeral lightness that had just found its way into his heart. He took a moment before responding, hoping not to scare them off with his acknowledgment. Hoping it was not all a figment of his imagination.

But he knew there was no way he could've imagined something so vivid. The air was too dense, the winds too cold, the skies too dark.

"Do you smell it?" he replied. He inhaled deeply, allowing the scent to fill his lungs and quell any doubts of its existence. "It's going to rain..."

After too many years of drought, it was finally going to rain.

Judging by their advance across the sky, the coming

storm would be a big one. Everything it hadn't rained in twenty odd years, every drop that had been held back in their drizzles, all of it would fall on them tonight. But they couldn't be caught out here for it. The desert was unforgiving with its heat, but its rains were deadly.

As if prodding them on, a sharp crack of thunder sounded above.

"Come, we've got to go," he added as he nudged the horse back into action.

"It's just rain…" Keziah called out to him, but he simply plodded on ahead. He had no idea how to explain to her that what she thought was "just rain" would lead to a river that would sweep them into the next ocean. It was best they got home before he startled her.

The echo of thunder followed closely on their heels. Even the horses sensed the impending downpour, pounding faster at the desert trail. When they arrived, the skies had darkened sufficiently for the streaks of lightning to shine through.

The old house, the hovel of stones slapped together and plastered with white clay, stood as a welcome sight. It wasn't the opulent manors he'd seen in the forest, but it was a home—his home.

The rain gutters were strewn across the floor haphazardly, waiting to finally be rehung.

His horse had hardly come to a halt before Caspar dismounted. He took hold of both leads and guided them towards the side of the house. A small stable, one so long out of use that the splintering wooden doors clung with their last shred of life to their hinges, waited for them. As he helped Keziah dismount, he couldn't help himself from stealing a kiss.

Soon, the winds picked up around them, tugging at their clothes and hair. The next crack of thunder shook the wooden rafters. The soothing scent of petrichor danced on the breeze.

New life blossomed in the air, and Caspar found part of it had blossomed within him as well.

The pair of them gazed up at the sky, watching as the first drops began to fall. When Caspar returned his focus to Keziah, he found her lips tilted in amusement. Her eyes sparkled under each flash of lightning, green and bright like burning copper. He brushed his thumb over her cheeks, removing a thin layer of desert dust from them, admiring the blush he found beneath.

She had no idea how beautiful she was—windswept and flustered from their ride, she still clung to her proud charisma, and he loved every second of it.

The drizzle began to pick up. The mares grew restless, warning their human counterparts that it was time to seek shelter. The water seeped into their garments, darkening the fabrics at their shoulders and arms.

"Weren't you afraid of the rain?" Keziah smirked as she traced her fingers over his chest.

"Afraid? No. Concerned? Slightly…" he said mockingly. "Can you blame me? The woman I love is prone to drowning."

"Hey!" she replied, poking at his chest. Before she could reply, a faint voice called out to them.

"Caspar…"

He turned suddenly.

At the edge of the property, his father stood trembling, a hammer in one hand, his cane in the other. With mouth agape, he stared at the lovebirds and the luxurious horses in his derelict stable. The shock had hit him hard, his cane barely holding him upright. Caspar had never seen his father in such a state. Time had marched on unfavourably in his father's lifetime, but he hadn't realized how broken the man had become. The fire in his eyes had long since been put out, gone the day his mother died. His hair had greyed and dwindled. No longer did he look like the soldier Caspar had painted him out to be. Now, standing before them, he was simply a crippled old man courting death.

"Father, we have returned," he said. He pulled Keziah in close, guarding her. He had no idea what to expect of his father after having run out on him.

To Caspar's surprise, tears disguised by the rain began to fall from his father's eyes. His father loosened his grip on the cane. His knees wobbled. He dropped the hammer he'd been carrying to the wayside, along with the cane. They fell unceremoniously to the dirt as his father hobbled over to them.

"Father, what are you—"

But his father cut him short, embracing Caspar with all his might.

"I am so sorry, my son," he said as he sobbed into Caspar's tunic. "Please forgive me…"

The world seemed to stand still. The only sound Caspar could hear was the beating of his own heart. He looked down at his father.

Has he always been this small?

"I never meant to drive you away… My son, I am so proud of you."

Caspar's heart stopped. *He's proud…of me?* The words broke one of the locks on his heart he hadn't realized he was harbouring. Slowly, Caspar wrapped his arms around his father's trembling body, the word *proud* ringing across his mind.

Another crack of thunder sounded overhead, rattling the walls of the surrounding canyons. This alone snapped Caspar out of his daze. Little streams had begun forming around them with the rains. By this time, they were all drenched, red mud splashing up over the hems of their garments.

"Father… It's time to go inside…" he whispered, already missing the fleeting moment. He hadn't realized it initially, but at some point, between seeing his father and their embrace, he'd started to shed tears of his own.

His father lifted his head from Caspar's chest and turned to face Keziah.

"Young lady," he called. Caspar was worried about what might come from his mouth, but once again, his father surprised him. "He's safe," he said feebly, placing a hand over his heart. "You brought him back safe."

Keziah smiled at him and replied, "It would appear we are better people than we thought."

Caspar had no idea what had transpired between the two of them, but they seemed to be in each other's confidences.

"We should all get inside. Quickly," Caspar said as he gathered the cargo from the horses' saddles. "The storm will not wait."

Caspar ushered them towards the house, but Keziah had other plans. She looked at him, a fire burning in her eyes that no rain could put out, and he knew instinctively what she was asking. She wanted permission to rain-proof the house. No sooner did Caspar give her a consenting nod did she work her magic.

The stable was fortified; the mares better protected from

the winds and rain. The rain gutters were lifted on pillars that grew directly from the ground, their mounting directing the water into a newly formed well. The streams formed by the storm were redirected away from the house to avoid flooding.

By the time she was finished, Keziah was soaked and coated in mud up to her knees, but she was happier than he'd ever seen her. His father too gazed on approvingly at her work.

The three of them hurried inside under the next sky-splitting streak of lightning.

A long time ago, Caspar's mother had told him that some of the prettiest flowers bloomed in adversity. A younger him hadn't understood at the time how that phrase would follow him into adulthood. But in her presence, suddenly everything made sense. The way two enemies could set aside differences to work for a common goal. How they could fall for each other between insults and arguments. And how, perhaps, such a love could uproot even the deepest of hatreds.

Caspar had set the tea to boil, all the while thinking about his mother's words. He watched as his father and Keziah began to exchange stories. A truce, tentative as it was, between the two of them was more than he felt he could've ever asked for.

And as the storm raged on beyond the walls of the old stone house, a garden was beginning to bloom within.

♠ EPILOGUE ♠

FOR THE NEXT FORTY DAYS, IT RAINED consistently over the Red Desert towns of the *Argia* nation. By that time, their world had changed. Underground aquifers were replenished. The village gardens overflowed with produce. The lemon trees dotting the town were practically toppling over with a swollen, bountiful harvest.

But the roses of the desert weren't the only buds blooming.

The storm had initially masked Keziah's presence from the townspeople, but by the time the rains softened, so had their attitudes towards her. During one of the worst nights of the storm, one of the reservoirs overflowed, threatening to topple the better part of the marketplace and all who lived nearby.

Cries for help filled the air. Homes were flooded. Livestock was lost. It was the greatest tragedy the town had ever experienced since the fires that had scorched their lands decades prior—and it would have been worse, had it not been for Keziah.

That evening, she'd finished making preparations for their own house, fearing the worst when her drainage systems began to overflow. She'd known it would only be a matter of time before the rivers decided to burst. That night, her worst fears were realized. By the time the first cry filled the night sky, she'd already taken off on one of the horses towards the centre. Caspar followed close behind knowing that, strong as she was, water would always be her weakness.

She set to work immediately, wading through rising streams to raise barriers of stone throughout the town. The initial terror at her being a *Harri kanala* quickly subsided once people realised that she was there to help. At first, they only watched, fearing proximity to her might put them in harm's way. But the strength of Keziah's spirit and her need to help was too powerful to ignore. Soon enough, the soldiers—even some who had tried to drown her—raced out to assist, using some of the smaller boulders she'd dug up to prop against windows and doors in an effort to keep the waters out. Rescues were happening all about the town. People were pulled from collapsing huts and saved from being swept away with the rains.

Many lives were lost that day, but many more were spared.

And it was all thanks to her.

By the time the rains let up, the town was a broken shell of its former self. The white clay walls of the houses had been stained red with the rich soils of the desert. In some cases, the watermarks went all the way up to the thatched roofs. It was as if over those forty days the town and its people had drowned in their own hatreds. What had remained bore no resemblance to the picturesque quaintness that had characterized it for decades prior. The cracks in the underlying foundations which the townspeople had tried to mask had been ripped open by the life-altering storm. All that was left was the memory and the grief, and even those would fade soon enough.

* * *

Caspar stared out the window at the rows of tomato plants whose leaves swayed lackadaisically in the breeze. Their swollen fruits glowed bright reds and yellows as they dangled on the vines. He filled a pot with water and set it to boil, humming softly to himself.

The morning sun had just begun peeking over the canyon walls, casting long shadows across the fertile red soils. Overhead, pink clouds dotted the skies, a stark contrast from the seas of grey that had blanketed them months prior.

The rainy season had ended.

The cold of the mornings had begun lingering into the later hours of the day. Winter was not yet upon them, but the evenings had become pleasant enough to sit outside unsheltered, accompanied by blankets and warm mugs of mint tea.

But the house was not as he'd once known it. Keziah had remodelled the derelict abode into something resembling a quaint cottage—humble, respectful, but with the small touches of luxury she'd been accustomed to in her own lands. She'd extended the existing structure, added bedrooms, and put a roof over the bathing house. The horses had a proper stable. The grounds had proper drainage. And, of course, she fixed the garden. She put her heart and soul into their small oasis at the edge of the desert, until it resembled every bit the gem she was.

The pot began to boil, summoning him from his contemplative stare. He added mint leaves, sugar, and green tea, stirring to keep the concoction aerated and lively. His mother, distant as his memory was of her, had always claimed that was the secret to good tea. To keep it lively, let it breathe as people do. Let it simmer as their hearts do. By the time it was served, it would no longer be the simple sum of earth and water. It would hold within it the secret to life itself… Or so she claimed.

Staring into the pot as he stirred, Caspar caught a glimpse of his reflection and smiled. Her eyes stared back at him. For a brief moment, he was taken back to the house before the storms, to the kitchen that smelled of dried spice and charcoal. Where she tousled his auburn locks as he sat on the countertop watching her cook.

The rains had brought back his memories of her. He pictured her clearer than he had in years. Caspar had been nothing but a boy when he'd lost her, but since the rains, the fog in his mind had settled. He remembered her— happy.

Caspar blinked away the nostalgia. With a deep sigh, he pulled the pot from the stove and poured the tea out into the mugs. The steam curled in the cool morning air, filling it with wafts of mint and sugar.

"Is that one for me?" Keziah asked mid-yawn.

She sidled up behind him and wrapped her arms around his torso. Warmth from their bed emanated from her body, spreading across his back as she tightened her embrace. He rested the pot down, careful not to burn her before spinning her around to face him.

Sleep crusted her eyes. Strands of dark hair stuck out at odd angles. She smiled up at him, and Caspar felt his heart melt. He smoothed out the tangles of hair before planting a kiss atop her crown.

"Hmm… Actually, I thought I'd give it to the vipers instead," he teased.

She stretched up and pulled his face towards hers. "You. Are. So. Funny," she replied, punctuating her words with light, fleeting kisses—save for the last one.

Caspar had taken the earlier kisses as jest, but that last one was a treasure. He held her closer, tighter. Kept her pinned between the counter and his body as he pressed his mouth against hers, deepening the kiss. Keziah sank into his arms as a moan slipped from her lips.

"Don't start… You know what happened last time…" he mumbled through the kisses.

As if on cue, a bouncing toddler appeared at their feet, wrapping himself around his mother's leg. Keziah smiled beneath the pressure of his lips before whispering, "We'll save that for later…"

Caspar planted another kiss to her forehead before bending over to retrieve their son. "Alright, Nuri, you little viper," he began as he tossed him into the air. The sound of Nuri's laugh echoed throughout the kitchen, ending the contemplative silence of the morning.

"Bobba," Nuri squealed with delight.

Keziah took the opportunity to relish in a few unincumbered sips of tea, watching them lovingly from over the lip of the mug. When he looked over at her again, Caspar caught a glimpse of fire twinkling in her eyes. It sent a shiver down his spine. Even after years together, he still could not get over the way his heart leapt at the sight of her. Even now, he thanked every star in the night sky for blessing him with that fruitless hunt and stray arrow.

"Shall we leave Ma to have her tea and go pick some tomatoes?" Caspar asked, nuzzling his son's stomach with his nose.

"Uhuh," came the reply.

"I'll start on breakfast," Keziah said, planting a kiss on both their cheeks before they headed out.

The crisp chill of the morning desert air welcomed them by raising goosebumps across their skin. Nuri's little hand clutched tight to his index finger as he stepped down from the stone foundation to the garden path. Caspar felt his grip tighten as he steadied his bare feet on the ground.

Caspar had long noted how Nuri liked the feel of the earth between his toes—like his mother. He had all the colourings of a *Harri*, but in spirit, he was all fire Caspar mused. The only parts of his child that looked like him were the mass of unruly curls atop his head and his sparkling, amber-coloured eyes. Caspar was consistently surprised at how alert he was for someone his age, how those little eyes widened like saucers as they marvelled at the wonders of the natural world. He himself could no longer remember the nuances of childhood but wondered as he watched his son whether he had been as curious. Those little hands reached for everything—leaves, fruits, stones, insects… Caspar worried his curiosity would get him into trouble one day, but he knew better than to stifle the curiosity.

Nuri released his finger and began to race through the stalks, his unspoken plea to be chased. The sound of childish laughter cut through the cold of the morning. A smile curled on Caspar's lips watching his little form push through the much larger foliage. He caught the occasional glimpse of jet-black curls through the green and made sure to stay a pace or two behind to keep up the illusion of chase.

Caspar ducked down like an animal on the prowl, ready to pounce on his little boy.

But Nuri had played this game before. The giggling stopped when he could no longer see his father's form through the stalks. Soon, even the swishing and the incautious footsteps stopped.

For someone so young, he'd already grasped the delicate nature of the hunt—*like his father*, Caspar mused. He gave him a second or two before resuming his hunt.

"Nuri..." he called as he crawled through the stalks. "Nuri..."

Normally, he'd get some sort of a chuckle out of him. Today, it seemed Nuri was able to hold his tongue. Pride flowed through him, until the third call, which was also met with silence.

Caspar paused, waiting to hear the softer chuckles beneath the rustling of the leaves. Nothing. He waited a breath, steadying himself to hear the lower tones of the world. Still nothing. Worry flooded his heart. Since becoming a parent, he finally understood his father's qualms. His gaze dropped to the soil, looking for a trail of tiny footprints. He'd lost a few to the scattered stones in the dirt but soon found relief in a steady trail that led to the edge of the garden.

Nuri had come to a halt beyond the foliage. His little body sat before the headstone, a small flame dancing in the palm of his hands. His eyes were fixed on the carved letters that spelled out his own name.

"Nuri?" Caspar called softly, his worry subsiding.

"Bobba," his little voice hesitated. "Where is Apa now?"

Caspar crouched down beside his son, patting his head as his gaze bounced from him to the stone. For a moment, he was reminded of a conversation between himself and his late father. That was the last they'd spoken of his mother until Keziah had entered their lives. Her headstone sat a mere foot away, worn down by the many years of his father's avoidance of the subject. In his later years, his father had taken to caring for it, claiming to have seen so much of his wife in Keziah that he'd been forced to reevaluate the distance he'd put between himself and her memory. Now, both stones sat solemnly in a memorial plot that Keziah had forced them all to tend to—to honour the way Iturri demanded, even if the corpses had been burned.

"He is with the stars," Caspar replied.

"Why have they taken him, Bobba?"

"Because he wished to be with Ama," he said, but he sensed his son was not content with such a response.

Nuri dropped the little flame and twirled his shirt between his fingers, shying away from the stones. "But why?"

Caspar opened his arms, allowing Nuri to fall into them. He scooped him up and plopped him in his lap, taking a seat before the stones. "One day, my little viper, we will all leave these lands and end up in the stars."

Nuri's little brow furrowed. "What if I don't want to leave? What if I am afraid?"

"*Ya haram*, there is no need to be afraid. We will all be together in the next life, and the one after that." As he spoke, his eyes drifted to Keziah, who was humming away in the kitchen. As if sensing his gaze, she looked up from her preparations, meeting his eyes with a gentle smile. "We will come back together again… We always do."

Nuri snuggled into his chest. "Bobba, can you tell me about Apa Nuri?"

All at once, Caspar's heart was overrun with emotion—melancholy, nostalgia, gratitude…and of course, love. It was hard to remember a time when these felt as foreign to him as the lands beyond the desert—and they might have remained that way, had it not been for a harsh season, a stray arrow, and a stubborn girl. Caspar mouthed the words, *I love you*, to her, and smiled when he received them in reply. When he turned back to the stones, his heart was so laden with emotion that he felt it clawing up his throat. He cleared it, preparing for the tale, and Nuri settled into him further.

"Once upon a time, there was a great hunter of fire who fell in love with a tree spirit…"

IF YOU LIKED THIS BOOK…

Please leave a review of it on your favourite sites. These reviews help small-time authors like me reach new audiences and are much appreciated!

If you'd like more from the world of Visanthe, check out the following books:

If you're a poetry fan, check these out as well:

And be on the lookout for more amazing books!

WANT MORE MAGIC?

The story doesn't end here. In fact, you've only gotten a taste of the world I've built for you. Join my inner circle of readers and unlock:

- Exclusive Bonus Chapters & Short Stories
- First looks at my next releases before anyone else
- Behind-the-scenes snippets
- …And many more surprises!

Sign up for my newsletter to gain access to all the fantasy and fun. And check out my social media to keep up to date with the madness behind the mind.

Find all the links at the page below:

https://linktr.ee/lmsanguinette

ACKNOWLEDGMENTS

What began as a simple palate cleanser turned into a full-fledged story of its own. It still baffles me, eight books in, that I am able to continue writing, let alone come back to this wonderful world. I'd like to thank all those who made it possible.

I extend my deepest gratitude to my editor, Cara, for her help and motivation both in the actual writing process and in the getting out of writer's block process. Thank you for having believed in me from my first book back in 2021, all the way to this one, my ninth book in four years. Without you, none of this would've been possible.

I'd like to also thank my constant supporters—who have since become friends—Marcia, Fae, Assia, Natalie, and Fiona. You girls are the reason I keep writing. The fact that you find happiness in the worlds I create and continue to seek more from them fulfils me deeply. For a long time, I believed no one else in the world would care for my stories or my characters as much as I do. You girls happily proved me wrong, and for that, I am forever grateful.

Next, I'd like to thank the friends who became family—Jade, Rachele, Gabrielle, Tessa, Sara, Sarah, and Kristel, for keeping me grounded throughout this endeavour. You girls took care of me in the moments of darkness which led to these beautiful books, so it would only be right to acknowledge the unseen support. Thank you, from the bottom of my heart.

And a special thanks goes out to one of my biggest supporters, and one of my best friends. Alexis, thank you for housing me and chauffeuring me around the U.S. for all the book fairs and allowing me to share a special part of my life with you. The way you get excited about my writing fulfils me more than you know. Thank you for pushing me forward along this journey, even and especially when I wanted to quit. I am so grateful to consider you a friend, and one that has seen every book fair thus far. A true champion.

Finally, I'd like to thank my family, for their love and support. To my mum, my biggest supporter, in all my writings. To my dad, for his pushing me to always do better. And to my siblings, for being the brightest lights in my life. I love you all.

ABOUT THE AUTHOR

L. M. Sanguinette was born on a small island in the Caribbean, where the palm trees watched over her like giants and the sea crept up to her feet to say hello. Ever since she was little, she surrounded herself with tales of fantasy and magic, hoping that one day, she too would be involved in a story like the ones that captured her imagination.

Years—and many rewatching's of Avatar the Last Airbender—later, she is happily living in the worlds that her mind created, filling her bookshelves with more books than she will ever read, and practising her own version of magic.

When she's not sitting at the computer, she can be found snorkelling near forgotten shores, twisting from silks that hang from the ceilings, or in one of the many hidden coffee shops of Madrid, conversing with the spirits of the old city and dreaming up new adventures.

9 781968 824020